THE COMPLETE
COMPUTER POPULARITY PROGRAM

TODD STRASSER

The Complete Computer Popularity Program

A YEARLING BOOK

Published by
Dell Publishing
a division of
Bantam Doubleday Dell Publishing Group, Inc.
666 Fifth Avenue
New York, New York 10103

ISBN: 0-440-40436-3

Reprinted by arrangement with Delacorte Press

Printed in the United States of America

March 1991

10 9 8 7 6 5 4 3 2 1

OPM

to George Nicholson

1

"I'm warning you, Cook," Paul Smerman said. "You may find Peekham very disappointing socially." The tall, bony seventh grader bent over a complicated-looking mess of electronic gadgets on the worktable in his basement as he soldered two wires together with a small soldering iron.

"Why?" asked Tony Cook, who was standing next to him, peering over his shoulder.

"I can think of at least four reasons," Paul said. "First, because you are new here. Second, because the seventh grade at Peekham Junior High has evolved into an extraordinarily cliquish and unfriendly class. And third, because your father is a safety engineer at the nuclear power plant and, as you have probably noticed, everybody in Peekham hates that plant."

Paul straightened up and unplugged the soldering iron. With his wild, uncombed dark hair, and clothes that seemed two sizes too small, he looked like a teenage mad scientist. Or a scarecrow with a high IQ.

"What's the fourth reason?" Tony asked.

"The fourth reason, Cook, is that you have already made the mistake of associating with me. That alone is probably enough to make you utterly unacceptable to the rest of the grade."

"I don't get it," Tony said. "You're not such a bad guy. And you must be one of the smartest kids in the grade, if not the whole junior high."

Paul nodded. "Thank you for the compliment. Unfortunately, here in Peekham intelligence has nothing to do with social acceptance. In the areas of deductive reasoning and computer science I may be far ahead of the grade. But socially I haven't made much progress since nursery school."

"Then this is the perfect time to catch up," Tony said.

"I'm afraid it's too late for that."

"Why?"

"It just is," Paul said as he bent over his contraption and started to work on it again.

As Tony watched, he decided that Paul must have been wrong. It was true that the Cooks had just moved to Peekham a few months ago and that his father was a safety engineer at the Peekham Nuclear Power Plant. But his father had been a safety engineer at the power plant in Connecticut before they moved, and Tony didn't remember anyone hating him for that. And while there did seem to be frequent antinuclear demonstrations here, there'd been antinuke demonstrations at the old plant too. It was something Tony and his family had simply got used to.

And why was Paul so negative about the kids at school? Tony had only been in school for a few weeks, but they didn't seem so bad. Why was Paul so convinced that they disliked him? Sure, he was a little strange. Weren't most superbrains? But there was nothing obnoxious about him. Actually, Tony was glad he'd found Paul, who'd gone to the same summer camp he had for the last two years. Otherwise, here in Peekham he wouldn't have known anyone his own age at all.

"Can you hold this for a second?" Paul asked, handing him a small flashlight and directing its beam into the depths of the miniature electronic junkyard. Looking more closely at Paul's contraption, Tony recognized a small speaker that might have come from a transistor radio. There was an old picture tube from a portable TV, and a used computer keyboard. But mostly there were wires. Wires going everywhere.

"What is this thing?" Tony asked.

"Top secret," Paul said as he probed deeply into the electronic innards with a screwdriver.

"Oh, come on," Tony said. "Who am I gonna tell? I don't know anyone in Peekham besides you."

"Doesn't matter."

"You're being ridiculous," Tony said.

"All right. What are you doing Friday night?" Paul asked, still hunched over.

"Uh, I don't know yet," Tony said. "And what does that have to do with this?"

"If you come over and help me work," Paul said, "I'll tell you."

"Wouldn't you rather go out someplace Friday night?" Tony asked. "Like the video arcade at the mall or the pizzeria? Maybe we could meet some kids."

"Impossible," Paul muttered.

"How can that be impossible?" Tony asked. "Kids hang around those places all the time."

Paul looked up from his contraption and over at Tony. His eyes narrowed. "Maybe I'm wrong about you, Cook. Maybe in a month you'll have a whole new set of friends and be part of some clique. One day we'll pass in the hall at school and suddenly you won't even remember my name. I'll just be one of the nameless outcasts, grouped with everyone else who's too fat or too tall or too ugly or too uncoordinated to be popular. Don't worry about it, Cook. It won't be the first time. Somehow it has been decided that my role in life is to be the first friend every new kid makes when they get here. They always hang around with me just long enough to find out who they really want to be friends with, and then I'm forgotten and sent back to the funny farm."

"Come on, Paul, I wouldn't do that," Tony said.

"Then how about helping me finish this thing on Friday night?"

"Well, okay," Tony said reluctantly. Spending Friday night in Paul's damp, chilly basement wasn't exactly his idea of a good time. But he really didn't have anything better to do. And besides, he didn't want Paul to develop a complex or anything.

2

The next day in Miss Crowe's class at school, Tony discovered that Paul's warnings were not all made up in his imagination. They were studying different kinds of energy: electric and solar, kinetic and potential, hydraulic and nuclear. Miss Crowe was a small woman who reminded Tony of a bird. Not a crow, though. She was more like a sparrow. When she talked, she chirped. She started the class by saying, "As you all probably know, the Peekham Nuclear Power Plant went into operation last fall. Does anyone know why today is significant?"

Around the room hands began to go up.

"Is it Thursday, Miss Crowe?" someone asked.

"Yes, but why is that significant?" the teacher chirped.

"Because it's the day before Friday," someone else said.

"Why is that important?" Miss Crowe asked.

"Because after Friday comes the weekend and

there's no school!" Several cheers went up around the room.

Miss Crowe rolled her eyes. "Class, today has a special meaning in relation to the nuclear power plant. Now, who is going to tell me what that meaning is?"

This time only one hand went up, and Miss Crowe called on Laurie Stone, the prettiest, smartest, and most popular girl in the grade. "They've been running the plant for one year," Laurie said.

Miss Crowe nodded. "That's right, Laurie. Today marks exactly one year since the power plant went into operation. How do you feel about that?"

Around the room more hands went up, and Miss Crowe picked Joel Hinkie, whose mother was one of the leaders of the antinuke movement in Peekham.

"Sooner or later there's going to be a nuclear accident and we're all going to be contaminated," Joel said.

Tony grimaced. Around his house he tried not to mention phrases like "nuclear accident" and "contaminated" too often. But in school they seemed more popular than curse words. And so were the kids who used them. If Laurie Stone was the most popular girl in the grade, then Joel Hinkie was one of the most popular boys. Laurie was tall and had long streaked blond hair and blue eyes. Joel was also tall, but his hair was light brown and curly (Tony had never looked closely at the color of his eyes). He'd heard that Joel and Laurie were going together.

Miss Crowe called on another student, who said the reactor could melt a hole straight through to China. More hands began to go up, and every single student

Miss Crowe called on was against the nuclear power plant.

As more and more kids spoke, Tony slouched lower in his seat. He was beginning to feel a little uncomfortable.

Miss Crowe kept asking for opinions. Tony felt someone poke him in the back. He turned around and glanced at Paul, who sat behind him.

"What do you want?" Tony whispered.

"Don't let them talk about the plant that way," Paul whispered. "That's where your father works."

"Cool it, Paul," Tony whispered, and turned around again.

Just at that moment Miss Crowe said, "So far, all of you have spoken against the plant. Won't anyone defend it?"

The room went silent.

"You mean you don't think there is *anything* good about nuclear power?" Miss Crowe asked.

It looked as if no one was going to answer. But then a hand went up behind Tony. And that hand belonged to a bigmouth named Paul Smerman.

"Ask Cook," Paul said, pointing at Tony. "His father works there."

Suddenly everyone in the class was staring at Tony. He felt his face begin to turn red.

"Is that true?" Miss Crowe asked. "Your father is employed there?"

Tony had no choice but to tell the truth. "Yes, he's a safety engineer."

"Safety?" someone said. "That's a laugh."

"I don't see how you can call nuclear power safe," said Laurie Stone.

"Wait a minute, class," Miss Crowe said. She turned back to Tony. "Do *you* think nuclear power is safe?"

Tony felt the eyes of the class upon him. This wasn't exactly the way he'd hoped the other kids would get to know him. But on the other hand, he had to defend what his father did for a living. Slowly he sat up.

"To tell you the truth," he said, "I think it all depends on how nuclear energy is handled. If it's handled safely, then it's probably safe. If it's handled unsafely, then it's probably unsafe. But I don't think that nuclear energy itself is inherently safe or unsafe."

In the next row David Dinks turned and gave Tony a mean look. Dinks was a seventh grader, too, but he was big enough to play on the varsity football team. He was about five feet six and weighed a hundred and forty pounds.

"I could *inherently* break your face," David Dinks grumbled, and a couple of kids snickered.

Tony tried to ignore him.

"But is it possible to believe that nuclear energy will always be handled safely?" Miss Crowe chirped. "Already there have been numerous accidents."

Tony nodded. "I guess scientists hope they'll learn enough from those accidents to prevent them from happening again."

"But if the next accident happens here in Peekham, we could be blown to smithereens," someone a couple of rows over said.

"Yeah, my mother says they built that stupid thing right on an earthquake fault," said Joel Hinkie.

"My father says if they don't shut that plant soon, we're moving," said someone else.

Tony felt as if a great dark mushroom cloud were settling right over his head. Every time someone said something against the nuclear plant, everyone looked right at him as if *he* were the local representative of the Peekham Power Company. They really *did* seem to hold his father's job against him.

3

_____

That afternoon Tony and Paul left school together. A lot of kids were waiting around in front for buses to take them home, and others were leaving on bicycles and skateboards. Tony had the feeling that all of them had someplace to go and something interesting to do. All of them except him and Paul.

"Why'd you have to tell them about my father?" he asked as they turned down the road from school and walked past the athletic fields.

"He works for the plant, doesn't he?" Paul said. He was carrying a big pile of schoolbooks and ring binders under one arm and a violin case in the other.

"Sure, but I don't see why it was so important to tell everyone in the class," Tony said.

"I suppose I thought you might present a different point of view," Paul said.

"You sure that's the reason?" Tony asked.

"What other reason could there be?"

"Maybe you were hoping that if everyone found out

what my father did for a living, they'd hold it against me," Tony said.

"Nonsense," Paul said.

For a while they walked down the road without talking. Tony wasn't sure he believed Paul, but it didn't really matter now. A couple of kids on ten-speeds raced past them, and Tony kicked a crushed beer can a couple of times until it bounced off the pavement and into a storm drain. Paul shifted the big pile of books and the violin, trying to switch them from one arm to the other.

"I still don't see why you're so convinced no one likes you," Tony said.

"It's not important, Cook," Paul said as he struggled with his books. "I accept my life. I'm a computer nerd, one of those people who relates better to machines than to other people."

"But it doesn't have to be that way," Tony said.

"Yes, it does," said Paul.

"I bet we could both be as popular as we wanted to be," Tony said. "The computer nerd and the nuclear kid."

"I don't care about being popular," said Paul.

"Bull," Tony said. "You do, but you just don't want to admit it. Everybody cares about what people think of them."

Suddenly Paul's books fell to the ground with a thud. Paul put the violin case down and started to rub his arms. "That's true," he said. "And I do care what *certain* people think of me. For instance, in a couple of weeks I'm going to care what the judges at the school science fair think of me, and in a couple of years I'm going to care very much that my teachers like me enough to give me fantastic recommendations for college. And someday I will want to know that my fellow scientists and colleagues both like and respect me. But why should I care if a bunch of junior high school students like me or not?"

"Because you're one of them," Tony said.

"An unfortunate coincidence," Paul said. "And something which I look forward to outgrowing."

"Everybody wants to be liked, Paul," Tony insisted.

"I said I agreed with that, Cook," Paul replied. "I simply disagree on *whom* we want to like us." He looked down at the violin case and the pile of books as if trying to decide how to get them home.

"You want me to help you carry some?" Tony asked.

Paul bent down and quickly started dividing the books into two piles. He gave one pile to Tony and kept the other for himself. Tony got the impression that Paul kept the lighter pile.

"A truly generous offer," Paul said as they started to walk again. Tony was certain he had the heavier pile.

They walked to Paul's, a small gray house on a crowded block. Paul's parents ran a grocery store in town, and Tony knew they didn't make much money. That was obvious just from the clothes Paul wore, which were always too small and looked as if they'd come from the Salvation Army. Tony carried Paul's books into the house and then turned to leave.

"You want to see my new IBM personal computer catalog?" Paul asked.

"No, I have to get home," Tony said. He took a few

steps toward the door and then stopped. "You know," he said, turning to his friend again, "I've made a decision about you. Either you are a very strange person, or you really do care what the kids in our grade think of you and you're just too scared to admit it."

Paul thought for a moment. Then he said, "I can only think of one suitable reply to that comment, Cook."

"What's that?" Tony asked.

"Whatever you decide to be when you grow up, don't be a psychiatrist."

Later, when Tony got home, he saw that his mother was in the garage. In the middle of the garage floor was an old blanket covered with a mountain of new blue jeans. Mrs. Cook herself was wearing jeans and a navy-blue sweater and was folding and marking each pair with a size and a price. Earlier that week she'd bought the jeans wholesale from a manufacturer in the city, and that weekend she would sell them at a flea market near Peekham.

"Well, look who's home from school," Mrs. Cook said. "Think you could help me for a little while?" She pushed at the red bandanna that kept her dark hair out of her eyes.

Tony really didn't feel like it, but he didn't have anything better to do. "Okay," he said.

"You fold and I'll mark," his mother said. Tony picked up a stiff pair of jeans and started to fold them.

"So, how was school today?" Mrs. Cook asked.

Tony shrugged. "Okay, I guess."

His mother looked up at him. "Something wrong?"

Tony picked up another pair of jeans. "I don't know."

"Hmm, sounds like something's wrong to me," Mrs. Cook said.

Tony looked across at her. "Mom, you think kids here wouldn't like me because Dad works at the nuclear plant?"

"What gave you that idea?"

"Well, Paul said they might," Tony said.

"Paul?" Mrs. Cook said. "Oh, yes, the boy you know from camp."

Tony nodded. "Yeah. And in science class today it looked like he was right."

"What happened?"

Tony explained how everyone in class had ganged up on him after they found out that Mr. Cook was a nuclear safety engineer. His mother stopped marking the jeans and listened.

"Well," she said when he'd finished, "I think it's unfortunate that that happened. But I don't believe that they'd really not like you just because of Dad's job. Look at Tim and Joyce. They've made friends." Tim and Joyce were Tony's older brother and sister. Tim was in ninth grade and Joyce was in eleventh.

"Yeah, but Tim's friends are all into music," Tony said. "They probably think a nuclear reactor is some kind of stereo component. And have you noticed how all of a sudden Joyce is antinuke, just like everyone else? Sometimes I think she just follows the crowd, Mom. Whatever they're against, she's against."

"I don't think that's true," Mrs. Cook said.

"Well, then how come she wasn't antinuke when we

lived in Connecticut and Dad worked in the nuclear plant there?" Tony asked.

"I suppose she wasn't as conscious of the issue then," his mother said. "And let's not stop folding. There's a lot to go."

Tony sighed and picked up another pair of jeans. He wasn't sure he believed that stuff about being conscious of issues. "You think it would be right if I became antinuke just so I could make more friends?" he asked.

"I don't see any reason why you can't make friends just the way you are," his mother said. "You're handsome and intelligent and a terrific kid."

"I'm short," Tony said.

"The doctor says you haven't had your growth spurt yet."

"When am I going to get it?" Tony asked.

"I don't know," his mother said. "But in the meantime, there's absolutely no reason why you can't make all the friends you want."

Tony shrugged. "You're just prejudiced."

"Of course I am," Mrs. Cook said. "Would you rather I wasn't?"

"Well, no."

"You know," his mother said, "maybe you haven't given it enough time. Sometimes it takes a while to make new friends."

"It hasn't taken Joyce and Tim much time," Tony said.

"Then maybe you haven't tried hard enough."

Tony nodded and continued to fold the jeans. Back in Connecticut he'd always made friends without having to try, and *trying* seemed like a strange idea, but maybe she was right.

4

————————————————————————

"Come on, let's just try it," Tony said the next day as he dragged Paul into the locker room. It was Friday, and Tony had decided that he and Paul were going to try to get into the after-school touch football game.

"But what's the point?" Paul asked as Tony pulled him past the rows of gray metal lockers.

"The point is that sometimes you have to try if you want to make friends."

"But what does making friends have to do with playing touch football?"

"Plenty," Tony said. "The only way you're going to make friends is by proving that you're more than just a computer nerd."

"But I *am* just a computer nerd," Paul said. "I'm happy as a computer nerd. I've accepted my fate. Why do this to me?"

"Because I don't believe you," Tony said.

Paul sat down on the bench in front of his locker and scratched his head.

"I think you will discover that you are making a mistake, Cook," he said as he started to do the combination on his locker, "if you think we are going to gain esteem in the eyes of our fellow students on the football field. Only morons excel in sports."

"That's a myth and you know it," Tony said impatiently. "Now stop stalling and let's go."

Paul shrugged and pulled open his locker. "Too bad, it looks like I don't have any sweat socks."

"Then wear your black ones," Tony said.

"Black socks with sneakers?" Paul said. "Isn't that considered bad taste?"

"Come on, Paul. Nobody cares what color your socks are," Tony said. "Besides, you could probably use the exercise."

Paul shuddered. "Don't mention that word to me, Cook. It makes me break out in hives."

Paul took forever to change clothes, and by the time Tony got him out to the athletic field, the captains had already started choosing up sides for the game. The touch football game on Friday afternoons was one of the major events of the week, and a lot of good athletes played in it. Joel Hinkie was one of the captains, and a wiry track-and-field jock named Robbie Carmichael was the other.

Paul and Tony joined the crowd waiting to get picked.

"I got Stein," Carmichael said, pointing at one kid.

"Then I got Williams," Joel said, pointing to another.

"Okay, I get Copelin," said Carmichael.

While he and Paul waited, Tony looked over at the

bleachers. Laurie Stone was there with some of her friends. One of them was a pretty girl with red hair named Randy Kahn, who worked on the yearbook. The other was a slim blonde named Stephanie McKearny, who was on the cheerleading squad. Seeing them, Tony began to feel nervous. Being on the short side and not weighing a lot, he'd never been a very good football player. It was going to be hard enough just playing the game. Knowing those girls were watching was only going to make it worse.

But first he had to get into the game. Tony suddenly realized that all the guys in the crowd had been picked for a team except him and Paul. And neither Hinkie nor Carmichael looked as if they were going to continue choosing.

"Uh, what about us?" Tony asked.

Joel glanced at him and Paul. "It looks like we got full teams."

"Yeah, but—" Before Tony could say more, someone yelled, "Hey! Look who's coming!"

Everyone turned and saw David Dinks lumbering toward them. All one hundred and forty pounds of him.

"I got Dinks!" shouted Carmichael, whose turn it was to pick.

"Aw, that's not fair," Joel complained.

But Carmichael pointed at Paul and Tony. "You can have both of those guys."

"Are you kidding?" Joel said, gesturing to Tony and Paul. "These two guys combined aren't worth half of a David Dinks."

"Tough," Carmichael said. He turned and took his team down to the other end of the field for the kickoff.

Joel looked at Paul and Tony. "Okay," he said with a shrug. "You're with us."

Tony and Paul looked at each other. It wasn't a great beginning, but at least they were on a team.

The game started, and the reason why Joel was unhappy about not getting Dinks on his team quickly became obvious. Each time Carmichael's team ran a play, the kid with the football got behind Dinks and followed as the human bulldozer knocked down players on Hinkie's team. Eventually one of Tony's teammates would manage to sneak behind and tag the ball carrier, but with Dinks doing the blocking, Carmichael's team made impressive progress. In fact, it was 21–0 in no time.

Meanwhile Joel's team didn't score a point. Each time they had the ball Joel would call some incredibly complicated play, like a double crisscross down and out or a reverse flea-flicker. No one on the team understood what he was supposed to do. As a result, everyone would just run around and hope he was doing the right thing.

About halfway through the game Joel called out a new play. "Let's try an end-run fake with a lateral screen option."

"Great," someone said. "What's that?"

Joel tried to explain what each player was supposed to do, but Tony could tell by the looks on their faces that they didn't understand. As usual, Joel had left Tony and Paul out of the play completely.

"What about us?" Tony asked as the huddle broke up.

"You guys go long for the bomb," Joel said.

That was no surprise. Hinkie had been sending Tony and Paul out for long bombs on almost every play. Of course, the long bombs were never launched.

A moment later Tony and Paul stood at the line of scrimmage and waited for Hinkie to call out the signals. When the ball was snapped, they both took off down the field, just as they had all afternoon. After a couple of seconds Tony looked back, expecting to find the play over. Instead, he saw a bunch of players from Carmichael's team chasing Hinkie behind the line of scrimmage. The end-run fake hadn't worked, and it looked as if Joel was going to be thrown for a huge loss.

Tony started to wave his arms. "Here!" he shouted. "Look here! Here!" Amazingly, Joel saw him and desperately heaved the ball. Tony watched it sail way up into the air. He realized that it was going to go over his head, but as he turned around he saw Paul ahead of him, still jogging along, oblivious to what was happening.

"Hey, Paul, look!" Tony shouted.

Startled, Paul turned around just as the ball fell out of the sky at him. He threw up his arms, mostly to protect himself. But the ball landed right in his hands. Paul fell over backward across the goal line and wound up sitting on the grass with the ball in his lap.

"Touchdown!"

"Unbelievable!"

"Super catch!"

Suddenly everyone on Joel's team was running down the field to congratulate Paul on his fantastic catch.

Tony was the first to reach him. "Paul, that was incredible! How did you catch it?"

Paul looked down at the ball as if he couldn't understand what it was doing there. "I honestly don't know, Cook."

But it didn't matter. A second later Paul was surrounded by the rest of Joel's team. He'd scored the first touchdown of the day. He was a hero.

5

Paul's catch changed the game. Joel's team got totally psyched up, while Carmichael's team was totally psyched out. No one on either team could believe that a brain like Paul Smerman had managed such an incredible catch. But that wasn't the end of it. Before the game was over, Paul caught two more passes and even scored another touchdown. Joel's team won, 49–35.

"You were great," Tony said. He and Paul stood on the field at the end of the game. The other kids had already started to leave.

"Well, I must admit that I did not expect to score two touchdowns," Paul said. "I think that random chance was very much in my favor today."

Tony rolled his eyes. "Anything you say, Paul. But you see, you're more than just a computer nerd."

"Maybe I'm a computer nerd who catches footballs," Paul replied.

Tony shook his head, and they started back toward the gym. But before they got very far they heard someone call out, "Hey, Paul!"

Tony turned and saw Joel waving at them from the bleachers. He was standing with a bunch of kids.

"Hey, Paul!" Joel yelled again. "Come over here."

Paul glanced at Tony. "What does he want?"

"I don't know," Tony said. "Let's go see."

They walked over to the bleachers where Laurie and her friends were sitting. Joel and a couple of other guys from his team were standing around in front of them, leaning on the railing.

"You made a couple of great catches," Joel said.

"I think it was mostly luck," Paul said. Tony was acutely aware that the whole crowd was looking at them. He kept glancing at Laurie and Randy and their friends. Girls definitely made him nervous.

"But it really drove them bonkers," Joel said. "Turned the game right around for us."

Now Laurie turned toward them, her long streaked blond hair falling over her shoulders.

"I didn't know you played football," she said to Paul.

Paul blushed. "Well, I'm not certain I did, either."

"You were good," Laurie said.

"Uh, thanks," Paul mumbled, and started to look around nervously.

"See you at next Friday's game, okay?" Joel said.

Paul nodded and suddenly turned away. He started walking so fast that Tony practically had to jog to catch up to him.

"How come you didn't stay and talk?" Tony asked.

"I don't know," Paul said as he headed toward the gym. "I guess I didn't think they wanted to."

"What do you mean? They complimented you, didn't they?"

"But that doesn't mean they wanted to have a conversation," Paul said.

"Oh, come on, Paul, sure they did," Tony said.

They entered the locker room, and Paul quickly began to change out of his gym clothes. Tony stood beside him, watching.

"Paul," he said. "You can't prove to them that you're not a computer nerd if you don't talk to them. I bet they're really curious about you."

"Because they think I'm some sort of freak, probably," Paul muttered.

"No," Tony said. "Because you've revealed a whole other side of yourself that no one ever suspected you had. That's interesting, Paul. You're interesting."

Again Paul didn't answer him. Tony sat down on the bench in front of his locker and started to do his combination.

"You'll play next week, right?" he said.

"I doubt it," Paul replied.

Tony stared at him. "Why not? Joel asked you to come back."

"So does my dentist every six months."

"I don't understand you," Tony said. "You had a good time. You played well. You got to mess around with a bunch of other guys. You even got to talk to some girls. Don't you care about that?"

Paul stood up and started buttoning his plaid shirt. "Listen," he said, "let me remind you that touch football is a game. It can be classified with other games, like baseball and handball, and even tiddledywinks, for that matter. Now, it just so happens that games count for very little in the broad scope of things. Do you really think that whether or not I get asked to play touch football again next week matters in comparison to the technological future of this country? I mean, can you picture some Nobel Prize–winning scientist turning to his associate on the other side of some lab and saying, 'Hey, I just heard that Paul Smerman was asked to play touch football next week'? I mean, why would they care?"

"You're missing the whole point," Tony said. "We're not scientists. We're in the seventh grade. We've got six years of junior high and high school to go. Do you really want to go through it like some kind of hermit?"

Paul started tying his shoes. "What I don't understand is why it's so important to you that I be involved in this. Why can't you leave me out of it? If you want to make friends with Joel Hinkie and his crowd, go right ahead."

Tony shrugged. "They probably think that if they become friendly with me, their chromosomes will start to mutate or something."

"And you think *I'm* weird?" Paul asked.

Tony looked down at the locker room floor. "I just thought that maybe it would be easier and more fun if we tried together. That's all."

Paul closed his locker and picked up his schoolbooks. "A hopeless effort, Cook. But look at it this way. We can always be hermits together."

6

The idea of spending the next six years being a hermit with Paul did not appeal to Tony. Nor did the idea of spending the next six years worth of Friday nights in Paul's musty, damp basement working on his secret invention. But Tony didn't have anything better to do, so after the game he went back to Paul's house and down to the basement.

Paul turned on the light and pulled a plastic cover off the miniature electronic junkyard.

"Are you going to tell me what this thing is?" Tony asked.

"If I tell you, you must swear that you will tell no one, absolutely no one," Paul insisted.

Tony glanced up at him. "What's the big deal?"

"I am going to win the junior high science fair with this 'thing,' as you call it, and I can't risk anyone stealing my idea," Paul said.

Tony looked down at the secret invention. It was such a mess of wires and gadgets and transistors that he doubted anyone would *want* to steal it. "Sure, Paul, I won't tell anyone."

Paul smiled and patted the TV tube gently. "It's a voice synthesizer," he said proudly.

"A what?"

"It talks," Paul said. "It will say anything I want it to say."

Tony looked at the thing more closely. How could a bunch of junk held together with wires talk?

"Watch, Cook," Paul said. He flicked a switch next to the computer keyboard. Some lights went on and the TV screen lit up.

"I type on the computer what I want it to say," Paul explained. "It's programmed with more than a hundred basic phonetic sounds, so it can say almost anything."

"Oh, great," Tony said. "Now all you have to do is teach it to dance and you'll have a date for the junior high ball."

Paul smirked. He typed something on the keyboard, and a second later a weird electronic voice came through the speaker: *"Cook doesn't believe I work."*

Tony was shocked. "How'd it do that?"

Paul smiled. "I told you, Cook. It's speech synthesis. A miracle of the computer age."

Tony stared at the voice synthesizer. "Let me try it." He reached toward the keyboard. He was taking typing at school and was getting to be pretty good.

Tony typed, and the synthesizer spoke again in its weird synthetic voice. *"Don't look now, Paul, but your fly is open."*

Paul looked down. "I knew you'd find a practical application for it, Cook," he said, zipping his fly.

Tony stepped back and stared at the speech synthesizer. At camp he had always known that Paul was really smart, but now he was beginning to suspect that the kid was a true genius. The whole thing was made out of old junk—and it worked! Unreal.

"Did you really invent this yourself?" he asked.

"Well, there have been other speech synthesizers before this," Paul admitted. "But you can say nearly anything on this one. It has almost zero phonetic limitations."

Tony nodded. A homemade speech synthesizer. And to think it was made by the same kid who'd caught two touchdown passes.

Paul turned off the synthesizer and put the plastic cover back on so it wouldn't collect dust.

"Demonstration over," he said. "Let's go upstairs."

Tony followed him into the kitchen, which was small and cramped. The house was old and had a funny smell, like dirty clothes that had been left in the hamper too long. While Paul looked around for something to eat, Tony stood by the kitchen window and watched a couple of kids on the street outside throwing a football around. That reminded him of something.

"Could you believe the way she complimented you?" he said.

"Who?" Paul asked, as he looked through some cabinets.

"Laurie Stone."

"Oh, no." Paul groaned. "Don't start that again."

Tony turned away from the window. "But didn't you see how surprised she was that you were a good football player?" he asked. "She's probably just as curious about you as you are about her."

"Who said I'm curious about Laurie Stone?" Paul asked.

"Oh, come on, Paul, tell me you're not interested in the smartest, prettiest, most popular girl in the grade," Tony said.

"At the moment I'm considerably more interested in food." Paul pulled out a jar of peanut butter. "Want to have peanut butter and lettuce sandwiches for dinner?"

"Why don't we go out for pizza?" Tony said, trying to think of an excuse to go someplace where something sociable might happen.

"Well, uh . . ." Paul checked his pockets. "I only have forty cents."

Tony sighed. "Okay, forget it."

"Tell you what, Cook," Paul said. "Pizza sounds like a good idea. My parents have these new frozen pizzas on French bread at the store. I'll run down and get a package of them if you'll set the table."

Tony frowned at him. "Set the table? To eat pizza?"

"Of course," Paul said, as if it were the most normal thing in the world.

Tony decided not to argue. If that's the way they did it at Paul's house, it was okay with him. But frankly he thought a couple of paper towels were all they needed.

Paul left, and Tony started looking for the silverware. But he kept thinking about Laurie Stone and how friendly she'd acted after the football game. A lot friendlier than she'd been in Miss Crowe's class the day they'd talked about the nuclear plant. If only there were some way he could talk to her, Tony thought, without her knowing he was the kid whose father worked at the plant. . . . Wait a minute. What about the synthesizer? It talked, but Laurie would never recognize that voice.

He still had some time before Paul would get back with the pizza, so he went downstairs to the basement. Fortunately he remembered most of what Paul had said about using the computer. There was a phone down there and he called information and got the Stones' number. He dialed it and put the receiver next to the synthesizer's speaker. Then he sat down at the keyboard and waited nervously.

"Hello?" someone answered.

Tony quickly typed, and the synthesizer spoke in its electronic voice. *"Is Laurie there?"*

"This is Laurie. Who's this?"

Again Tony quickly hunted for the correct keys. *"A friend."*

"Who are you?" Laurie asked. "You sound weird."

Tony typed furiously. *"I talk through a computer. But you know me. Can I ask a question?"*

"Wait," Laurie said. "Who is this? Is this an obscene phone call?"

Tony almost panicked. *"Not obscene,"* he typed. *"I'm shy."*

"Are you sure this isn't an obscene phone call?" Laurie said. "I've always wanted to know what one sounded like."

"I don't know how to make an obscene call," Tony typed on the synthesizer.

"Oh." Laurie sounded disappointed. "How do I know you really know me?"

That was a good question. Finally Tony typed, *"You're beautiful and intelligent."*

Laurie laughed. "Okay, you've convinced me. Now, what do you want?"

"What does it take to make friends?" he typed.

"What? That's a weird question. I don't know, I don't even know who you are," Laurie said.

That's a problem, Tony thought. Then he typed, *"In general?"*

"Oh, I don't know," Laurie said. "Hey, is this some kind of joke?"

"No joke," Tony typed. *"I'm serious."*

"Are you someone who wants people to like her?"

Her? Tony thought. Then he realized that Laurie couldn't tell whether it was a boy or a girl calling. The electronic synthesizer voice had no gender.

"Hello?" Laurie said.

"Still here," Tony typed.

"This isn't Sheila Carter, is it?" Laurie asked.

"Don't guess," Tony typed. *"What about making friends?"*

"I've never really thought about it, whoever you are," Laurie said. "I mean, it's not a big deal."

"Not for you. You already have friends," Tony typed.

"But there's nothing to it," Laurie said. "If you don't

pick your nose in class or wear weird clothes, you're ninety percent there."

That was a problem, Tony thought. As far as he knew, Paul didn't pick his nose in class, but he did wear some pretty weird clothes.

"No problem with the nose. I can work on the clothes," Tony typed.

"And you can't be obnoxious," Laurie said.

"I agree," Tony typed.

"Somehow you don't seem obnoxious," Laurie said. "Let's see. Obviously you're someone who doesn't have many friends. Now why would that be?" She began to name the possible reasons. "You don't have disgusting habits. You're not obnoxious. Are you just plain boring?"

"I hope not," Tony typed. He was pretty sure he wasn't boring. As for Paul, it seemed as if he was getting more interesting all the time.

"Hmm." Laurie paused for a moment. "I can't think of any other reason why you wouldn't be popular. Are you sure there isn't something you're not telling me?"

Of course there was, but Tony couldn't tell her that his father was a safety engineer at the nuclear power plant. And he couldn't tell her that his only friend was a superbrain football receiver who was convinced he was a nerd. Because then she'd know who he was.

Tony was just about to type another question when he heard the front door open upstairs.

"Cook?" Paul yelled. "Cook, where are you? The table isn't even set."

Tony didn't know what to do. He didn't want Paul to

catch him using the synthesizer, but he didn't want to stop talking with Laurie, either.

"Cook, where are you?" Paul yelled. Tony could hear the footsteps above as Paul searched around for him. He quickly typed *"Sorry, I have to get off now"* on the keyboard.

"Wait," Laurie said. "If you won't tell me who you are, at least give me a hint."

The footsteps were getting louder.

"I played football today," he typed.

Suddenly the door to the basement opened. Tony turned the synthesizer off and threw the cover over it. Paul was coming down the stairs.

"Cook, what are you doing down here?" Paul asked. He was carrying the package of frozen pizza.

"I was, uh . . . looking for silverware," Tony said.

Paul scowled. "In the basement?"

"Uh, sure," Tony said. "That's where we keep our silverware. Doesn't everyone?"

Paul stared at him. "And you think *I'm* weird?"

7

It rained all Saturday, and Tony spent most of the day around the house. He played home video games, read car magazines, and watched television. He called Paul's, but Mrs. Smerman said Paul had gone to the city to a computer show. He wondered what Laurie and Joel were doing. Probably fooling around at the mall with their friends, or at a movie, or something. Somehow it made the things he was doing seem less interesting.

Around the middle of the afternoon he wandered into the kitchen. His father was heating a pan of milk on the stove. Mr. Cook was a short, stocky man with black hair who made hot chocolate the old-fashioned way— instead of just emptying a packet of instant mix into a cup and throwing the whole thing into the microwave oven for thirty seconds.

"Want some?" Mr. Cook asked.

"Sure," Tony said, and sat down at the kitchen table. His mother was standing near the kitchen window, looking out at the pouring rain.

"Looks like the whole weekend's a washout," she said to Tony's father. "I hate the idea of being stuck all winter with three hundred pairs of jeans."

"Don't worry," Mr. Cook said. "There are still a few weekends before the flea market closes."

"But it's getting colder, and people don't like to come out," Mrs. Cook said.

"Just think," Tony said. "If you kept all those jeans, you could go almost a whole year without wearing the same pair twice."

His parents looked at each other.

"Where did we find him?" Mrs. Cook asked.

Mr. Cook shrugged and went to the bottom of the stairs. He yelled up toward Tim's and Joyce's rooms, "Anyone want hot chocolate?"

A voice yelled, "Yeah!" It was Tim. A few seconds later footsteps thundered down the stairs, and Tim appeared, wearing jeans and a yellow Who T-shirt. His shaggy brown hair was falling into his eyes.

He patted Tony on the head. "Hey, T-bone, how ya doing?"

"Okay. How about you?"

"Can't complain," Tim answered, and sat down at the table.

"Get us some mugs, Tony," Mr. Cook said as he took the hot chocolate off the stove.

Tony went to get the mugs out of the kitchen cabinet. He'd noticed lately that whenever his parents wanted something done or needed some help, they generally asked him. Probably because it was easier than asking Tim or Joyce, who might argue or give them a fight.

Tony got the mugs, and Mr. Cook poured out the hot chocolate. "Hey, Mom," Tim said. "Can I go to the late show at the Peekham Quad tonight? They're showing a Who movie."

"I don't think so, Tim," Mrs. Cook said. "You'll be out too late."

"Aw, Mom, all my friends are going. Their parents let them stay out late."

"If the movie starts at ten, Tim, you won't be home until midnight," Mrs. Cook said.

"Come on, Mom, I've stayed up till midnight before."

"I said no, Tim," Mrs. Cook said.

Tim looked disappointed, but he didn't argue anymore. The star arguer of the family was Joyce, who now sauntered into the kitchen wearing jeans and a black T-shirt with a white skull and crossbones on it and NO NUKES stenciled underneath. She was also wearing black nail polish with little white skulls and crossbones painted on. Tony was surprised she didn't have little white skull-and-crossbones barrettes in her hair, or maybe a gold skull and crossbones implanted in her front tooth.

Joyce leaned against the kitchen counter and stared at the rest of the family as if they were monkeys at the zoo.

"How quaint," she said with a mild sneer. "The family having hot chocolate together."

Mrs. Cook looked up at her. "Joyce, must you wear that T-shirt in the house?"

"Yes, I must."

It seemed to Tony that Joyce spent most of her time

lately looking for fights. He figured that she had chosen to wear the NO NUKES T-shirt just because she knew it would upset their father.

"You know, Joyce," Tim said. "I think you're antinuke just because that's what's fashionable at school. I mean, if it was fashionable to be against the water department, you'd probably be antiwater."

"You're so stupid, Tim," Joyce said. "There's no way you can compare water to nuclear energy. Water can't kill you, nuclear energy can."

"You could drown," Tony said.

Joyce made a face at him. "Yes, you could drown. But to drown you'd have to go swimming. If there was a nuclear accident, you wouldn't have to do anything except sit there." She looked at Mr. Cook. "Right, Dad?"

Mr. Cook turned and looked at Joyce. "You know, it's my job to see that a nuclear accident does not occur. And anyway, there have been nuclear power plants in this country for more than twenty years and there has not been a single death directly attributable to radiation. Have you got any idea how many people have died in coal mining accidents, natural gas explosions, and oil-tanker accidents in the last ten years? The number must be in the hundreds."

"But just one nuclear accident could kill hundreds of thousands of people," Joyce said.

"The chances of that kind of accident occurring are more than a billion to one," Mr. Cook said.

But Joyce only made a face at him. "You and your

stupid numbers." She sneered and then turned and left the kitchen.

Mr. Cook sighed and gazed up at the ceiling. "Ah, the joys of having a teenage daughter," he said wistfully.

"What's with her?" Tim asked. "She's such a downer all the time."

"It's just a stage she's going through," Mrs. Cook said. "I hope you'll remember what a downer your sister was when you get to be that age."

"All she does is fight with everyone," Tony said. "I don't see what she has to be so angry about."

No one answered him, and several minutes passed while they just sat at the table and sipped their hot chocolates. Then Tim got up and said he was going to practice his guitar. Mrs. Cook also left the kitchen, leaving Tony and Mr. Cook alone at the table.

"I don't know why people make such a big deal about the nuclear plant," Tony said to his father. "I mean, it's not like it's the only one in the world."

Mr. Cook looked across the table at him. "Your mother said you'd had some trouble at school about my job. Is it over now, or is it still a problem?"

Tony was surprised. He hadn't thought his mother had told his father about it.

"I mean," his father said. "No one really bothers you about that, do they?"

Tony looked up at his father and realized something. Being a new nuclear safety engineer in a town that was as antinuke as Peekham probably wasn't easy. Maybe it was as hard for his father as it was for him. Maybe even harder. Tony decided that the last thing his father needed was to hear about his problems. He probably had enough of his own.

"Nobody bothers me about it," Tony said.

Mr. Cook nodded. "I'm glad to hear that."

8

Laurie Stone and Randy Kahn sat next to each other in Mrs. Kellison's typing class, and on Monday Tony overheard Laurie tell Randy about a mysterious telephone call she'd got. Tony was sitting two seats behind Randy and could just barely hear.

"It was the weirdest thing," Laurie said in a low voice, leaning across the aisle toward Randy. "She was talking through some kind of machine. I think she called it a voice synthesizer or something. She wanted to know how to make friends."

"Do you know who she was?" Randy asked.

Laurie shook her head. "All I know is she said she plays football."

Tony bit his lip and kept listening. But before Laurie could say anything more, Mrs. Kellison came in.

"All right, students, please turn to page eighty-six of your typing manual." Mrs. Kellison was a tall woman with short hair who wore dresses that reminded Tony of Indian tepees. She tried to be very strict and didn't allow anyone to fool around in her class.

"Come on, no dawdling," she said. "I want to hear those typewriters clacking."

Tony started on the typing exercise. He wasn't exactly sure why he was taking typing. His mother said it was important for him to develop skills. Tony agreed with her, but the kinds of skills he was interested in developing were more like auto mechanics or graphic design than typing. Unfortunately the only class he could fit into his schedule was Mrs. Kellison's.

About halfway through the period Mrs. Kellison got up from her desk and said she had to go down to the office to take care of something.

"Just continue with your assignments, and I'll be right back," she told the class.

Everyone nodded, but as soon as she left the classroom every typewriter stopped. A spitball war broke out on the other side of the room. A couple of kids started drawing on the blackboard, and a bunch of girls gathered in the back to try on each other's makeup. Mrs. Kellison may have insisted on good behavior when she was in the classroom, but that only increased the temptation to mess around when she left.

Laurie and Randy leaned toward each other and began whispering again. Tony took a car magazine out of his book bag and pretended to read it while eavesdropping on their conversation.

"Going to the dance with Joel?" Randy asked as she took out a brush and pulled it through her red hair.

"I don't know, I guess," Laurie replied.

"You don't sound excited."

"I'm not."

"Why?"

"I always go to dances with Joel. I mean, he's nice and good-looking, but he's always there. Know what I mean?"

"Just part of the same old crowd?" Randy said.

"Exactly. I'd like to meet some new people."

"Why?"

"I don't know. I guess we've been with the same group of kids since kindergarten. I always thought that when I got to junior high there'd be some new faces around."

"There are a few," said Randy.

"Like who?"

"What about that guy, Barry Bates, who transferred here last year? He's cute."

"Get serious," Laurie said. "He hardly comes up to my chin."

"Well, what about Paul Smerman?"

Tony almost fell out of his chair.

"You think anyone could tear him away from his computers?" Laurie asked with a giggle.

"Would you want to?" Randy asked.

"I don't know," Laurie said. "He's so weird. Did you ever see the clothes he wears? I think I'd die before I went anywhere with him."

"Did you know he played football?" Randy asked.

"Are you kidding?" Laurie said. "I didn't even know he could run." Both girls giggled. Then Laurie gave Randy a look. "What about you?"

"And Paul Smerman?" Randy asked. "I hardly come up to his elbows."

"You mean his elbow patches," Laurie said.

Just then a kid near the door yelled that Mrs. Kellison was coming back down the hall. Everybody got back to their seats and quickly started typing. But Tony couldn't concentrate. He wished he could have tape-recorded that conversation. Boy, he'd love to see Paul's face when he played it for him. Imagine two of the most popular girls in the grade talking about him! And Tony got the feeling that if Paul ever started dressing normally, they might do more than just talk too.

9

Tony and Paul had different classes before lunch, and Tony usually got to the cafeteria first and waited for his friend before getting into line. That day he and Paul got in line and found themselves behind the massive bulk of David Dinks. In front of Dinks were Joel and Carmichael. All three of them were talking about the dance coming up on Saturday.

Behind them Tony was trying to listen.

"So what exciting things did you do this weekend?" Paul asked.

Tony quickly turned and brought a finger to his lips. "Shh."

Paul scowled. "Cook, what's wrong with you?"

"Be quiet," Tony whispered. "I'll explain later."

As the line moved everyone picked up a tray and set it on the silver rail that went past the glass cases where the cafeteria ladies gave out food. Tony tried to stay close to Dinks and his friends, but he kept his head turned away so it wouldn't be obvious that he was eavesdropping.

"You taking Laurie to the dance?" Dinks asked Joel. The human bulldozer had already started stuffing a hot dog into his mouth.

Joel shrugged. "I don't know."

"What's the matter?" Carmichael asked. "Doesn't Laurie like to dance?"

Joel smiled. "Yeah, she likes to dance. I just don't know if she likes to dance with me. She's been kind of cold to me lately, and I've been thinking I might ask Randy Kahn instead."

Standing on the other side of Dinks, Tony inched forward, trying to take in every word.

"Bet Laurie'd have a fit," Carmichael said.

"Yeah, well . . ." Joel lowered his voice and said something Tony couldn't hear. Dinks chuckled. Tony pushed his tray closer.

"You know what I heard?" Dinks said. Then he, too, dropped his voice. Tony strained forward to hear what he was saying, but Dinks was talking in a whisper. Tony slid his tray closer . . . and then a little closer. And then . . .

"Oooff!" He bumped into Dinks's back and bounced off.

Joel, Carmichael, an l Dinks looked around.

"Uh, sorry," Tony saiα, and quickly slid his tray back.

"Hey, it's the kid who glows in the dark," Dinks said. "Your old man blow anyone up lately?"

"No, dimwit," Tony said, angered by Dinks's crack.

"Hey, feisty little guy," Carmichael said.

"Yeah, and I don't like being called a dimwit," Dinks grumbled, stepping ominously toward Tony.

But Joel reached over and grabbed him. "Leave him alone, Dinks. He's half your size."

"Yeah, but he's got an oversize mouth," Dinks complained.

"To go with your undersize brain," Tony shot back.

Joel and Carmichael laughed, but Dinks made a fist and pointed it at Tony. "You better watch it," he threatened.

Tony smirked and let Dinks and his friends go ahead. He still hadn't picked out what he wanted for lunch.

Paul slid his tray up. "A command performance, Cook. Although I don't imagine it will help you make friends."

Tony shrugged. "You're right, but I just didn't like him making fun of my father."

He and Paul slid their trays toward the cashier. Joel and Carmichael and Dinks had already gone down to the table where they always sat, in the back of the cafeteria. Tony began to think again about what they'd said about the dance. He had an idea.

"Doing anything after school today?" he asked Paul.

"The mathematics society is having a meeting," Paul said. "We're going to discuss logarithms."

"Sounds exciting," Tony said.

"Not to you, obviously," Paul said.

"Your parents both at the store in the afternoon?" Tony asked.

"Usually," Paul said. "Why do you ask?"

"Oh, I was just wondering," Tony said.

Tony knew that what he was doing was totally wrong. Totally against the law. Totally crazy. If he got caught, he was certain his parents would ground him for the rest of the year, if they didn't send him away to a military school. Nevertheless, that afternoon after school Tony sneaked around to the back of Paul's house, pulled open one of the basement windows, and eased himself slowly inside.

It was dark in the basement. Tony swore to himself. The least he could have done was bring a flashlight or some matches. He inched across the floor, his arms outstretched, feeling for anything that would help guide him toward a light switch. His foot hit something, and there was a loud thud as it fell against the floor. Tony froze. He assumed there was no one in the house, but was he certain? How did he know that both of Paul's parents were at the store? What if one of them had stayed home that day?

For a long time Tony stood motionless in the dark, not moving a muscle, listening for a sound from upstairs. Finally he decided to take another step.

"Whoops!" He lost his balance and hit the floor with a smack. Now he was flat on his face on the basement floor. What an idiot! He'd tripped over the same dumb thing he'd knocked over before. He slowly got to his feet and started groping around again. Finally he touched something that felt like the staircase. Now he had his bearings. He took two steps to the right and started waving his arms around until he felt the string attached to the overhead light.

He pulled it and *presto!* Light! Tony looked across the

floor and saw that he'd tripped over an old stool. He went back and righted it. Then he went over to the speech synthesizer.

As he pulled off the dust cover, he figured he had at least an hour before Paul got home. Paul's parents usually kept the grocery store open until seven, so he probably didn't have to worry about them, either. He sat down in front of the synthesizer, turned it on, and dialed Laurie's telephone number.

"Hello?" It sounded like Laurie.

"It's me," the electronic voice said as Tony typed.

"My mystery caller, right?" Laurie said.

"Right."

"What are we going to talk about today?" Laurie asked.

"I know something."

"What?" Laurie asked.

"J. Hinkie will ask another to the dance."

"Really?"

"Yes," Tony typed.

"Whew, what a relief," Laurie said.

Tony was surprised by her reaction. *"But I thought you and he were . . ."* He wasn't sure what to type next.

"I know," Laurie said. "Nearly everyone thinks he and I are . . . something. But we're not. Who is he going to ask?"

"Randy Kahn," Tony typed.

"I can't believe it!" Laurie gasped. "She's one of my best friends. You must be wrong. How do you know?"

"I know."

"I can't believe it," Laurie said again.

"Why not?"

"Well, I don't care who he takes to the dance, but not one of my best friends," she said. "That's not fair."

"But you don't want him to ask you."

"Oh, I guess you're right," Laurie said. "I just wish he'd pick someone else."

"Someone not in the same old crowd?" Tony typed.

"Wait a minute," Laurie said. "How do you know about that?"

Tony didn't know how to answer. He couldn't tell her he'd listened to her conversation with Randy Kahn during Mrs. Kellison's class that afternoon.

"Hey, this is weird," Laurie said, sounding upset. "How do you know about all this stuff?"

"I just do. Don't get upset."

"But it's creepy," she said. "I feel like you must follow me around all day."

"Not true."

"You sure?" Laurie asked.

"Positive."

"What else do you know?"

"Not much," Tony typed. *"You think you'll still go to the dance?"*

"I guess. I don't know. I have to think about it," Laurie said. "Do you know why Joel's going to ask Randy?"

"Because you've been cold to him."

"That's because he's too serious," Laurie said. "My mother says I'm too young to have a steady boyfriend, and I think she's right." Laurie paused for a moment and then said, "Do you have a steady boyfriend?"

Tony frowned. Did he have a what? Then he remembered that Laurie thought he was a girl. *"Not at the moment,"* he typed back.

"My mother dated the same boy all through high school and got married when she was eighteen. She says it was a real mistake. They got divorced when I was five. Were either of your parents divorced?"

"No. They're the originals."

"My stepfather's okay," Laurie said. "Stephanie hates her stepfather. Do you know Stephanie?"

"She's the cheerleader."

"She made me swear I wouldn't tell anyone, but she has the worst crush on Robbie Carmichael," Laurie said. "Do you like any of the boys at school?"

A crazy idea flashed into Tony's head. Why not? he thought. Then he typed, *"I think Paul Smerman is very interesting."*

"Wow, that's the second time today someone's mentioned him," Laurie said. "Do you really like him?"

"He's different," Tony typed. *"He's a genius and a very good athlete."*

"But he wears such weird clothes."

"I don't think clothes are that important. The person in them is important."

"You're right," Laurie said. "I shouldn't care so much about what clothes someone wears. There are some boys I know who dress really nicely and are real jerks."

"Definitely."

"You know, I really like talking to you," Laurie said. "Won't you tell me who you are?"

"Maybe someday."

"But if you won't tell me, then I can't call you. I'll always have to wait for you to call me."

Tony had to admit that it was tempting to tell Laurie who he was. The only problem was that if he told her who he was, she might not want to call him.

"What about another hint?" Laurie said. "I don't even know what to call you."

"Call me Syn."

"What!?"

"Like in synthesizer," Tony added.

"Oh." Laurie laughed. "So tell me, Syn. Are you going to the dance?"

"I'll go if you'll go," Tony typed back. He noticed that a small red light on the computer console had begun to blink on and off, but he didn't know what it meant.

"Okay, that's a deal," Laurie said. "But how will I know that you're really there?"

Tony started to type something, but suddenly the synthesizer said, *"I blip urp simble you."*

"What?" Laurie said.

Tony couldn't figure out what the synthesizer had done. The little red light had stopped blinking and was now on full-time. He typed again. This time the synthesizer said, *"Prip on zip buddle."*

"What's going on?" Laurie asked.

Tony didn't know. But now he smelled smoke. Uh-oh. Something was really wrong. That's what the red light meant. Tony quickly turned off the synthesizer. He hated to do it, but he hung up on Laurie too. The smoke was coming from behind the TV tube. Tony got up, pulled the plug out of the wall socket, and backed away from the machine. He didn't know what to do. Was it going to explode? He looked around for a fire extinguisher but didn't see one.

Luckily, the smoke seemed to be stopping. Tony waited until it stopped completely. Then he threw the plastic cover back on the synthesizer and climbed out the basement window.

Tony couldn't concentrate on his homework that night. The memory of the smoking synthesizer was driving him crazy. You didn't sneak into your best friend's basement, destroy his most prized invention, and then just vanish into thin air. It just wasn't right. It wasn't fair to Paul. Tony knew he had to tell him the truth, even though Paul would probably call the cops on him.

He got up and dialed Paul's number.

"Hello?"

"Paul, it's Tony."

"Oh, Cook, how are you?" Paul asked. He didn't sound very upset.

"Oh, I'm okay. How are you?" Tony asked.

"Okay. What do you want?"

"Uh, well, uh, how was your mathematics meeting today?" Tony asked.

"It was fine, thank you," Paul said. "Since when do you care about my mathematics meetings?"

"Oh, uh, I was just asking," Tony said. Maybe Paul hadn't even discovered the damaged synthesizer yet, he thought. "Hey, how's your synthesizer working?"

"Just fine, Cook. It developed a short in the wiring tonight, but I fixed it pretty easily. Now, is there anything else you would like to know?"

Tony didn't reply, he was so relieved.

"Cook?"

"Yes," Tony said.

"You still there?"

"Uh, sure." Now that Tony knew the synthesizer was okay, he had another idea. "You know, if you become a world-famous scientist someday, it's going to be important that you know how to dance."

"What are you talking about?" Paul asked.

"When you get invited to those awards dinners and black-tie balls for winning the Nobel Prize," Tony said. "You're going to have to dance."

"Wait a minute," Paul said. "Is this another one of your schemes for making us popular?"

"Well, uh . . ."

"Or let me put it another way," Paul said. "Isn't there a junior high dance this Saturday?"

"Gee, that's right," Tony said in mock surprise. "What a coincidence!"

Paul chuckled. "You know something, Cook? You're about as subtle as a dead skunk."

10

It rained that Friday, washing out the after-school football game. But Tony didn't mind. It was the dance on Saturday night that he was really looking forward to.

He planned to sleep late on Saturday, but his mother had a surprise for him.

"I want you to help me at the flea market today," she said early in the morning as she shook him out of his sleep.

"But I have to get ready for the dance tonight." Tony yawned and tried to roll over.

"You'll have plenty of time to get ready later," his mother said, pulling down his blankets.

Tony rubbed his eyes. "What about Tim or Joyce? Why can't they go?"

"Because Tim has to help your father around the house and Joyce is busy," his mother said.

Tony sat up on the side of his bed. Busy? he thought. The only thing Joyce was busy at was being too much of a pain to have around the flea market all day. It wasn't fair. If you were loud and uncooperative you got out of working because nobody wanted to have you around. But if you kept your mouth shut and did what you were told, you wound up having to work.

After breakfast Tony helped his mother load the jeans and a folding table and chairs into the station wagon, and they drove to the racetrack where the flea market was held every weekend. The track was closed, but the owners rented out spaces in the parking lot and people came from all over to buy and sell clothes and household stuff at cheap prices.

It was a cold and cloudy day at the flea market, and Tony and his mother spent most of it in the lawn chairs drinking coffee and hot chocolate. They were wearing heavy sweaters, jackets, and hats. In front of them the table was piled high with the blue jeans Mrs. Cook wanted to sell before winter. But at the rate at which they were selling, it looked as if she was going to get stuck with a lot of them.

The problem was that they were all the way down at the end of the racetrack parking lot, away from what Tony's mother called the high-traffic area. Only about a third of the people who came to the flea market that day would bother to walk all the way down to their table.

"This isn't as good as the spot we used to have at the flea market in Connecticut," Tony said as he watched a mother with a couple of little kids stop and look at the jeans.

"I know," Mrs. Cook said. She sipped some steaming coffee from a plastic cup.

"How come we couldn't get a better spot?"

"Because we're new here," his mother said. "It takes years to get a good spot. When you're new at a flea market, they always give you the worst spots. You have to start all over again."

It's like making new friends, Tony thought.

The mother with the little kids left without buying any jeans. She had managed to leave several pairs unfolded and lying in the wrong piles, and Tony had to get up and refold them and put them in their correct places. Some people were really inconsiderate that way. They'd look at ten pairs of jeans and then just leave them lying anywhere.

"How about some music?" Mrs. Cook asked when Tony finished folding.

Tony nodded and went into the station wagon to get his tape player.

"The Beatles?" his mother asked. They were her favorite group.

"How about Van Halen?" Tony asked. The Beatles made him ill.

"Flip you for it."

Tony took a quarter out of his pocket and flipped it. Mrs. Cook called heads and won. Tony reluctantly put on a Beatles tape and wished he had brought earplugs. *"Michelle ma belle . . ."*

Mrs. Cook looked up at the cloudy sky. "Feels like rain."

"Want to start packing up?" Tony asked, eager to get out of the cold and away from the Beatles.

"Let's wait a little longer," his mother said. "We still might sell a few more pairs."

Tony nodded and sat back in his chair. He wondered what Paul was doing today. Probably in his basement working on his voice synthesizer. And Joel and Laurie? Joel was probably playing football with his friends somewhere, and Laurie was probably at the mall with her friends. Tony glanced up at the sky. A heavy black cloud was drifting slowly toward them.

Come on, rain, he begged. Gimme some big fat raindrops so we can get out of here.

"Will these shrink much?" someone asked.

Tony looked across the table and blinked. Stephanie McKearny was holding up a pair of jeans. Near her at the table, Laurie Stone was looking through the piles.

"Uh, uh." Tony tried to answer, but the words wouldn't come out.

"About half an inch at the waist and an inch in length," Mrs. Cook said.

Stephanie held the jeans against her hips and studied how far they fell. "What do you think?" she asked Laurie.

"I think they'll look really good," Tony said, standing up.

Both girls turned and looked at him.

"Don't I know you?" Stephanie asked.

"Yeah, I'm new at school," Tony said.

"You're a friend of Paul Smerman's," Laurie said.

Tony nodded.

Stephanie glanced at Laurie and then at Tony. "Is Paul going to the dance tonight?" she asked.

"I think so," Tony said. "But I can't say for sure. He's not really big on dancing."

The two girls looked at each other. "It doesn't really matter," Laurie said. They began looking through the piles of jeans again.

"Are you going to the dance?" Tony asked.

Laurie and Stephanie nodded. "Uh huh."

Tony grinned nervously. "Well, maybe I'll see you there."

Both girls smiled. "Maybe," Stephanie said. Then they walked away toward the next spot in the flea market, where a man was selling old record albums. Tony sat down next to his mother again.

"Friends?" Mrs. Cook asked.

"I wish," Tony said.

"And I wish you could have gotten them to buy some jeans," his mother said.

11

That evening after dinner Tony started to get ready for the dance. He put on jeans and a blue shirt and a navy-blue blazer, and he thought he looked fairly passable. At least he wouldn't stand out like a nerd or anything.

In the bathroom he looked at himself in the mirror. The one thing he wished he had was some hair on his face. It was something he'd noticed about the popular guys in his class. Some of them were starting to get dark hairs on their upper lips and even some whiskers on their chins. Tony wondered if there might be a correlation between facial hair and popularity. Maybe because it made them look more mature or something.

But what would he look like with whiskers? Or even a mustache? It was hard to imagine, but then Tony had an idea.

Taking two toothbrushes from the toothbrush holder next to the sink, he held them against his upper lip with the bristles pointing out. There. Even though he'd never have a white mustache, it gave him a general idea.

Suddenly there was a knock on the door, and it began to open. That was one of the problems with their new house. There was only one bathroom upstairs for Tony, Tim, and Joyce to share. To prevent unnecessary traffic jams, his parents had made a rule that they were not allowed to lock the bathroom door unless privacy was absolutely necessary.

Tony managed to pull the toothbrushes away from his face just as Joyce stepped in. She stopped abruptly. "Isn't that my toothbrush?"

Tony looked down. He had one toothbrush in each hand.

"Uh, yeah."

"What are you doing with it?"

"I was comparing them," Tony said. "You know, the weight and balance and grip. I'm thinking about changing brands."

Joyce looked at him as if he were crazy and then started putting on makeup. She was wearing her NO NUKES T-shirt again. They looked at each other in the mirror.

"Going to the dance?" Joyce said with a slight sneer, as if dances were beneath her.

"Yep," Tony said.

"Who're you going with?" Joyce asked as she applied purple eyeshadow.

"Paul."

"Sounds romantic," Joyce said.

Tony watched as she leaned close to the mirror and started applying a heavy dose of mascara to her eyelashes. "What are you doing?" he asked.

"Going to a no-nukes concert at the Coliseum," Joyce said.

"Sounds romantic," Tony said.

Joyce stopped making up for a moment and stared at her little brother. "It's for the cause," she said. Then she looked back into the mirror and started rubbing blush onto her cheeks.

"Is the makeup for the cause also?" Tony asked.

"Since when did you get to be such a wise guy?" Joyce asked.

Tony shrugged. "I was just asking, that's all."

"All the girls my age wear makeup," Joyce said, working on her face some more.

Tony sat down on the side of the tub and watched her. She really had changed a lot. It seemed to Tony that only a couple of years before she had been just another kid like Tim and him. They used to play together all the time. Then one day, like magic, she was no longer a kid. Now she wore makeup and bras and went on dates and had fights with their parents. It was hard to believe she was the same person.

"Do you remember junior high?" he asked.

"I try not to," Joyce said.

"Were you popular?" Tony asked.

Joyce turned and looked at him. "Is that what you're into now? Being popular?"

Tony shrugged and picked at a pebble in the tread of his sneaker. "It looks like I'm more into *not* being popular."

Joyce sat down next to him on the side of the bathtub. "Listen, Tony," she said. "Worrying about being popular is so dumb. I mean, think about what's going on in the rest of the world. We could have a nuclear war tomorrow and the whole earth would be destroyed. What would popularity mean then?"

Tony had no answer to that.

"You know what you should do tonight," his sister said. "Instead of going to that stupid dance, you should come with me to the concert."

But Tony shook his head. "I want to go to the dance."

"Why?" Joyce asked.

" 'Cause that's where everyone's going," he said.

"But it's so silly," Joyce said. "Worrying about popularity and going to dances just because everyone else is going. It's just a phase, Tony. Someday you'll think it was the dumbest thing you ever did."

Tony stood up. "Maybe I will. But how do you know that being antinuke and going to no-nukes rallies isn't just some dumb phase too?"

"Impossible," Joyce said. She turned back to the mirror and started working on her makeup again.

12

Later, at the Smermans' house, Paul opened the front door wearing a black suit that was two inches too short in the arms and the legs. He was also wearing black shoes and a white shirt and a wide green tie. His hair wasn't combed, and it stood up off his head like a potted fern.

Tony looked down at Paul's feet. Several inches of white sock were visible around his ankles. "Well, I guess you found your sweat socks."

"I didn't have any clean dark ones," Paul explained.

"You know, we're going to a dance, not a funeral," Tony said.

"I'm not sure I know the difference," Paul replied.

Tony smirked. "Okay, let's go."

"You sure you don't want to change your mind?" Paul asked as he stepped out of his house. "There's still time."

"Come on, Paul," Tony said. "Don't make it sound like the only reason you're going to this dance is for me."

"Why not?" Paul asked. "You think I'd go if you weren't forcing me?"

They started to walk down the sidewalk toward school. Tony looked up at Paul. "How am I forcing you?"

"Peer pressure," Paul told him. "I can feel it descending around me like a thick fog."

Tony shook his head. "You may be a genius, Paul. But you are also a nut."

Paul laughed. "Look who's talking. A kid who believes that the most important thing in life is being asked to play touch football on Friday afternoon."

They got to school early. The only kids around were a couple of tough-looking guys hanging out in the parking lot, smoking. Paul and Tony decided they'd better go inside. At the door they had to fork over three dollars each.

"I can't believe I have to pay for this torture," Paul grumbled, looking at the back of his hand where it had been stamped with blue ink.

"Try to think of it as a learning experience," Tony told him, as they walked into school.

"Why? Am I going to be graded?" Paul asked.

The gym was decorated with balloons and streamers. The bleachers had been shortened to just a few rows on each side, and along the back wall was a long refreshment table where teachers and monitors were setting up bowls of food and punch. A portable stage had been erected on the other side of the gym, and Tony noticed that a couple of musicians were setting up their instruments. He was surprised to see that they were the same guys who sometimes hung around his house playing music with his brother. In fact, there was Tim now—on the stage!

"Hey, come on," Tony said, pulling Paul toward the stage.

"What? You've decided to leave?" Paul asked hopefully.

"No, that's my brother," Tony said. He ran over to the stage where Tim and the other members of the band were plugging in their guitars and tuning up.

"Hey, Tim!" Tony yelled.

Tim turned around and looked down at him. "Hey, T-bone."

"You didn't tell me you were playing tonight," Tony said.

Tim crouched at the edge of the stage. "I didn't know, man," he said. "The guitarist who usually plays with this band got sick at the last minute. So they asked me to step in."

"That's great," Tony said.

Tim looked around and then said in a low voice, "Yeah, well, wish me luck, man. You know I've just played a couple of parties before this. And this is the first time any of us have played a dance."

"Don't worry, you guys'll do fine," Tony said. "You're probably better than the guitarist who was supposed to play."

Tim nodded. "Thanks for the encouragement. I gotta tune up now. Talk to you later."

Tony watched his brother join the other members of

the band. Tim was a rock-and-roll-star-to-be. Incredible!

More kids began to arrive, and the gym was soon divided into the girls' side and the boys' side, with a wide expanse of polished wooden floor between them. This always happened at dances. Even when Joel and his friends showed up with their dates, the guys and girls separated and went to their respective sides. Joel came with Randy Kahn. Tony watched the girls' side but saw no sign of Laurie.

He also noticed that most of the guys were wearing either blazers or sweaters. The girls were divided between those wearing jeans or cords and those in skirts. Only one person in the entire gym was wearing a black suit and a wide green tie.

Tim's band began to play and they didn't sound half bad. In fact, they sounded pretty good. Not that anyone dared cross the floor to ask someone of the opposite sex to dance. That would take time and a lot of prodding by the teachers who were standing by. For now, only a few girls danced among themselves while the rest stood around or sat on the bleachers talking and giggling. On the boys' side the talk concerned sports, cars, and the whereabouts of Laurie Stone.

"You think she'll come?" Carmichael asked Joel.

Joel shrugged. "I'm here with Randy. I don't care what Laurie does."

Meanwhile, Tony was trying to give Paul an informal dance lesson.

"You see what those girls are doing?" Tony said, pointing to the other side of the gym.

Paul squinted at them. "I saw something like that on a National Geographic Special once," he said.

"Well, that's all you have to do," Tony told him.

"Just pretend I'm part of some primitive tribe?" Paul asked.

Tony sighed. "The way you're dressed, it shouldn't be hard."

By now the gym was pretty crowded, at least along the walls. The middle of the floor remained as empty as ever, as if anyone who dared venture into that no-man's-land would instantly be struck by lightning. Tim's band kept playing song after song, and Tony could see that his brother was disappointed that no one was dancing. As bad as he felt for Tim, Tony knew for *sure* that he wasn't going to be the one who broke the ice.

Who did break the ice would probably be up to Mr. Van Dusen, the gym teacher and dance monitor, who was walking down the boys' side of the gym trying to goad a few of them into going over to the girls' side and asking someone to dance.

Mr. Van Dusen, a short, husky man with a military haircut, was wearing a plaid jacket and a bow tie. He stopped near Joel's group. "Okay, Hinkie," he said in a deep voice. "It's up to you."

"Aw, come on, Mr. Van Dusen," Joel complained. "How come I always have to start?"

"Because you're too dumb to say no, Hinkie," Mr.

Van Dusen told him. "Now get over there before I boot ya."

In a matter of seconds Joel got two of his friends to join him, and the three of them marched silently across the gym floor, thus signifying the true start of the dance. Before they even reached the girls' side, another half dozen boys were also on their way over.

"The rites begin," Paul observed.

But Tony didn't hear him. He had just noticed that Laurie had entered the gym. She was wearing a black-and-red-striped dress and red tights, and her normally straight hair was wavy. She was practically the only girl at the dance wearing a dress, and Tony watched as a lot of the other girls started glancing at her and whispering to each other. He thought she looked great.

"Okay, Paul, there she is," he said.

"Who?" Paul asked.

"Laurie Stone, of course."

"Of course?" Paul scowled.

"Paul, she'd love to dance with you."

"You're out of your mind, Cook," Paul told him. "There's absolutely no way I am going to ask Laurie Stone to dance."

"Suppose I told you that I overheard her talking about you in typing class this week," Tony said. "And suppose I told you that I talked to her at the flea market today and she even asked if you were coming to the dance tonight."

"I don't believe you," Paul said.

"I swear it's true," Tony said, even though it was

actually Stephanie who'd asked about Paul at the flea market.

"Are you serious?" Paul asked.

"Would I kid you about something like that?" Tony asked.

"In a word, yes," Paul said. But just the same, Tony noticed that he was glancing across the gym at Laurie. There were a lot of kids dancing now, but no one had asked her yet.

Tony gave him a little push. "Go on, ask her."

Paul took a step, but then hesitated. "What if she says no?"

"She won't," Tony said. "I promise."

"You sure?"

"I'm positive," Tony said, giving his friend another push.

He watched as Paul timidly crossed the floor toward Laurie. Actually Tony was surprised to see Paul agree. He had expected him to put up more of a fight. Now he just had to pray that Laurie would say yes. He started cheering silently. Go, Paul, go! Say yes, Laurie, say yes!

Paul reached the other side of the gym, and for a while he and Laurie just stood and talked. Tony was afraid that Laurie was making up polite excuses to get out of dancing with him. But then Paul led her out to the dance floor.

Tony wasn't the only one who noticed this. Nearby, David Dinks said, "Look who's dancing with Laurie." Several guys from Joel's crowd turned and watched.

"It's that brain, Smerman," said one.

"Boy, is Joel gonna be ticked," said another.

Tony watched Paul and Laurie carefully. Incredibly, Paul turned out to be a reasonably good dancer. At least he seemed to keep in time with the music. The song ended, but Paul and Laurie stayed on the dance floor, chatting and waiting for the next song to begin.

Across the gym, Tony was feeling encouraged. This was exactly what he'd hoped for. Obviously Laurie was willing to dance with other guys besides Joel, and not terribly popular guys, either. Tony hoped that once the other girls in the grade saw them, maybe they'd become a little friendlier too. After all, if Laurie Stone did it, it had to be okay.

The next song began, and Tony watched as Paul and Laurie started to dance again. Now Tony began to think about dancing too. After all, he wasn't there just to make sure Paul had a good time. He looked around the dance floor. There was Randy Kahn, but she was with Joel. There was Stephanie McKearny, but Laurie had said that she had a big crush on Robbie Carmichael. Maybe it would be best to leave her alone too.

Tony considered some other girls, but his eyes kept going back to Laurie. Of all the girls at the dance, she was the one he wanted to dance with the most. But could he? Well, why not? If she'd dance with Paul, she'd dance with him, right? Not only that, but if it wasn't for Tony, Paul probably never would have come to the dance in the first place. Surely he wouldn't mind if Tony cut in for one dance.

The song ended and Tony took a deep breath and started across the floor toward Paul and Laurie.

"Hi, Paul," he said when he reached them. He glanced nervously at Laurie.

"Oh, hi, Cook," Paul said, wiping his forehead with a handkerchief.

Tony tried to appear confident and at ease as he looked at Laurie. He had never been this close to her before, and he was a little surprised at how much taller she was than him. Four inches at least.

"Do you think I could cut in for a dance?" Tony asked, looking from Paul to Laurie.

Laurie frowned. "Oh, I'm sorry, but we're in the middle of the most interesting conversation. Perhaps a little later, okay?"

Tony glanced at Paul, but he just shrugged. Tony had no choice but to go back to the other side of the gym and wait.

The next song started, and Paul and Laurie began to dance again. They didn't seem to be talking anymore, either. Instead, Laurie was smiling and Paul looked a little dazed, as if he couldn't figure out exactly what was going on, but was trying his best anyway.

Tony waited as a few more songs were played, hoping that Paul and Laurie might decide to stop dancing on their own. But they didn't. It was hard to believe, but they just kept dancing, song after song. Finally he decided to cross the dance floor again.

This time when he tried to cut in Paul said, "Gee, I was just explaining radio astronomy to Laurie."

"But, Paul—" Tony started to say.

Paul cut him short. "In the name of science, Cook."

Tim's band started playing a new song, and Tony

returned to the boys' side again. This time Joel and his friends were waiting there for him.

"What does your friend think he's doing?" Joel asked.

"What does it look like?" Tony said.

"But Smerman?" Joel said. "I didn't think that guy could do anything except think. I mean, look at the clothes he's wearing. The guy's a joke."

Tony didn't like Joel's attitude. "I guess we're all just full of surprises," he said.

"Why don't you go cut in on him?" Dinks asked Joel.

"I can't," Joel said. "It wouldn't be fair to Randy. And Laurie probably wouldn't dance with me anyway."

So Tony and Joel and Joel's friends stood around and watched Paul and Laurie dance. All of a sudden Tony realized that he was being included in their group. At least he was standing around with them, and nobody had told him to get lost or anything. He looked around at Joel and Carmichael. This was almost as good as dancing with Laurie.

Then Carmichael said, "Hey, who is that band anyway? They're pretty good."

"I've never seen them before," Joel said.

"That's my brother's band," Tony said. Joel, Carmichael, and Dinks turned and looked at him.

"*Your* brother's band?" Dinks asked.

Tony nodded.

Joel glanced at the band again. "Which one is he?"

"The lead guitarist," Tony said.

"I've been watching him," Carmichael said. "He's got his stuff down pretty good."

"I'll tell him you said so," Tony said.

"You know, I play guitar too," said Joel.

"No kidding?" Tony said.

"You think your brother would show me how to do a couple of those licks?" Joel asked.

"Uh, sure," Tony said. "Anytime you like."

Joel nodded and then looked back toward Laurie and Paul. "Well, I guess I better go ask Randy to dance again before she starts wondering what's wrong," he said.

Joel started across to the girls' side, leaving Tony wondering. He hadn't made a big deal about asking if Tim would show him the licks sometime. He'd acted as if it were the most natural thing in the world. Tony wasn't certain what it meant, but he got the distinct feeling that Joel was being friendly to him.

13

_____

Later Tony tried unsuccessfully to cut in on Paul and Laurie once more, but they said they couldn't be disturbed because they were immersed in a passionate discussion about air pollution. Tony didn't argue, but it looked to him as if they were spending a lot more time smiling at each other than talking.

Tony did dance a couple of times with some other girls, but his thoughts were distracted. His best friend had double-crossed him.

After the dance was over, he and Paul walked along the sidewalk in the cool October air.

"Some friend you are," Tony grumbled.

"What?" Paul asked dreamily.

"The plan called for you to dance a couple of times with Laurie and then I was supposed to get a chance," Tony said.

"What plan?" Paul asked.

"My plan," Tony said.

"You never told me you had a plan," Paul said. "You just told me to go dance with Laurie."

"Yeah, but that was just to build your confidence," Tony explained. "Then you were supposed to go dance with some other girls."

"You should have told me," Paul said.

"Well, why do you think I kept trying to cut in on you two?" Tony asked.

Paul considered this and then said, "To tell you the truth, Cook, Laurie didn't seem that interested in dancing with you."

"That's because you didn't give her a chance," Tony said.

"How do you know she would have danced with you if I had?" Paul asked.

"Because, obviously, if she danced with you, then she isn't against dancing with slightly unpopular guys."

"Oh, no, not this again," Paul groaned.

"Well, it's true," Tony insisted.

"Okay, Cook, at the next dance, you can ask her to dance first," Paul said.

"Paul, the next dance isn't until the spring."

Paul didn't say anything, and they walked down the dark sidewalk in silence for a while. Finally they got to Paul's house, and Tony said, "Well?"

"Well, what?" Paul asked.

"Do you realize now that you're not just a computer nerd?" Tony said. "I mean, not only are you a genius and an interesting person, but you're a good athlete and a good dancer too. What more do you want?"

"I want to win the science fair next week," Paul said.

"I'm sure you will," Tony told him. "And in the

meantime, I bet you could even ask her out if you wanted."

"Who, Laurie?"

"No, Miss Piggy," Tony said.

"Why would I want to ask Laurie out?" Paul asked.

Tony couldn't believe him sometimes. How could anyone be so thick and so smart at the same time?

"Because it's obvious she's interested in you," Tony said. "I mean, she did dance the whole night with you."

"Cook, your sense of logical deduction astounds me," Paul said. "Just because we danced together does not mean we are starting a romance. As you pointed out, her regular beau came with another date. And she herself said I was one of the few guys in the grade tall enough to dance with her."

Then in the light of the Smermans' stoop Paul inspected his black suit.

"You know," he said, "perhaps I do need some new clothes."

"What makes you say that?" Tony asked.

"Laurie sort of hinted that this suit looked a little small on me," Paul said.

"She did, huh?" Tony said. "I thought you didn't care about things like clothes."

Paul seemed to fumble for words for a moment. "I don't really, Cook. But on the other hand, it wouldn't hurt to look presentable, would it?"

Tony smirked. "Of course not, Paul."

"Well, see you." Paul started to reach for the door, and Tony turned to walk back to his house. But before he got off the porch, Paul called out behind him.

"Cook."

Tony stopped. "Yeah?"

"Thanks for getting me to go to the dance. It probably is important for me to keep up with the latest steps. For my future as a scientist, that is."

Tony wanted to laugh. "Sure, Paul."

14

The morning after the dance Tony was upstairs in his bedroom looking through a car magazine and thinking about the night before. He was beginning to doubt that Paul was as oblivious to his social life as he pretended to be. Why else would he suddenly be talking about new clothes? Up until now Paul had simply worn whatever was in his closet.

Tony had to admit that it was ironic how things had turned out. It seemed as if he'd done all the work and Paul had got all the glory. After all, he was the one who had persuaded Paul to play touch football. He was the one who had called Laurie with the synthesizer. He was the one who had listened in on Laurie and Randy's conversations. He was the one who had got Paul to go to the dance. And Paul never would have asked Laurie to dance if Tony hadn't coaxed him.

And what was the result of all his hard work? Laurie had danced all night with Paul while he watched from the side.

The phone rang downstairs. "Tony!" he heard his mother yell. "Phone for you!"

Who could it be? Tony wondered as he jumped off his bed and went down to the kitchen. Probably Paul, calling to see if he wanted to go over and do advanced geometry problems on his computer. In the kitchen Tony picked up the phone. "Hello?"

"Tony? This is Joel."

"Joel?"

"Yeah. How're you doing?"

"I'm doing okay, Joel."

"You have a good time at the dance last night?" Joel asked.

"Uh, not bad," Tony said. "You?"

"Eh, it was okay," Joel said. "I thought your brother's band was pretty good."

"Yeah?"

"Yeah. You think I could come over and get him to show me some stuff on the guitar?"

"Today?" Tony asked.

"Well, I mean if it's okay," Joel said. "If you're too busy we could do it another time."

"Uh, no, I'm not too busy. Not at all," Tony said. "Come over whenever you want."

"Hey, that's great," Joel said. "See you in a little while."

After Joel hung up, Tony stood by the kitchen phone and didn't move. He couldn't believe it. One of the most popular guys in the grade had called him up and asked if he could come over. Just like that! As if they'd been friends for years or something. Tony shook his head. Amazing.

Since Joel was coming over, Tony decided he'd better clean up his room a little. He went upstairs and was making his bed when Joyce stopped in the doorway. She'd just got up and was wearing the long white T-shirt she usually slept in.

"What are you doing?" she asked with a yawn.

"What does it look like I'm doing?" Tony asked back.

"It looks like you're making your bed," Joyce said. "Are you feeling okay?"

"Very funny," Tony said. "But it just so happens that I'm getting ready for a friend to come over."

Joyce smiled. "A girlfriend?"

"Nope," Tony said, picking up a pair of sneakers and throwing them into his closet.

Joyce scowled. "A boy, I mean, *male* friend?"

"Yup," Tony said.

Now Tim joined Joyce in the doorway. He was wearing a pair of light-blue pajama bottoms. "Hey, T-bone, what are you doing?"

"He's making his bed," Joyce said.

"Wow, T-bone, what's wrong?" Tim asked.

"Nothing. Someone's coming over, that's all."

"You never made your bed when someone came over before," Tim said.

"Well, this is different," Tony said. "By the way, he wants to know if you'll show him how to play some stuff on the guitar, okay?"

"Sure," Tim said. "But who is it?"

"Joel Hinkie," Tony said.

"Who?"

"He's one of the most popular guys in my grade."
Tony tucked in the corners of his blanket.

"Tony is in his popularity stage," Joyce said.

"Yeah," Tim said. "I remember when you went
through that too."

"That's a lie," Joyce snapped. "I never cared about
stupid things like that."

"Yes, you did," Tim said. "I remember how you used
to cry when you didn't get invited to the right parties."

"That's not true!" Joyce yelled.

Tim laughed. "Oh, yes, it is!"

"You don't know what you're talking about, jerk!"
Joyce yelled at him and stormed away, leaving Tim in
the doorway. He pushed some of his shaggy hair out of
his eyes.

"So you figure if you make friends with this dude
everything will be cool, huh?"

Tony nodded as he pulled his blanket tightly across
the mattress. "Up till now I've only had one real friend
in Peekham," he said. "It's not like you and Joyce, who
have tons of friends."

"I don't have any real friends here," Tim said.

Tony stopped working on his bed for a moment.
"Sure you do. What about all those guys you hang out
with, and the guys you play music with?"

"They're friends all right," Tim said, leaning in the
doorway. "But they're not real friends. I mean, a real
friend is someone who you can really depend on, and
who you know will help you out if you get into trouble.

You're talking about someone you could tell your secrets to."

Tony was surprised. "And you don't have any?"

Tim shook his head. "I know a couple of guys who maybe someday will be real friends. But that takes time, man. I mean, we've only been living here a couple of months, right?"

Tony nodded. He'd never thought of it that way. If he used Tim's definition of a real friend, then he already had one. Paul.

"But you can't just have one real friend and forget about everyone else," Tony said.

"Probably not," Tim agreed. " 'Cause if you did, you'd get tired of him really fast. But remember, one real friend is worth a ton of not-so-real friends."

15

Later Joel came over with his guitar, and he and Tony went up to Tim's room. Tim was really nice about showing Joel how to play stuff, and they even played a couple of songs together. Tony, who didn't play an instrument, sat on Tim's bed and listened.

After a while Joel had learned everything he had wanted to know from Tim. As he and Tony were leaving Tim's room, Joel noticed that a door across the hall was open. He peeked in. "This your room?" he asked Tony.

"Yeah," Tony said, pushing open the door so Joel could go in. He noticed that Joel was looking at the posters of racing cars on his walls.

"You're into cars, huh?" Joel asked.

"Yeah," Tony said.

"You know, Randy Kahn's father collects old racing cars," Joel said. "They've got this big old barn in their backyard and it's full of cars."

"No kidding," Tony said.

Joel nodded. "Yeah, you ought to go over there and see them sometime."

Tony didn't say anything, but he didn't see how he could just invite himself over to Randy's like that. To Joel it seemed like nothing unusual. Just like it was no big deal to come over to Tony's house that day. Joel was confident that he'd be welcome anyplace he wanted to go. Tony could only wonder if he'd ever feel that way too.

Suddenly Joel looked at the radio-alarm clock on Tony's dresser.

"Hey, is that the right time?" he asked.

"I think so," Tony said.

Joel started looking around quickly. "Oh, man, the Dallas game must've started already. You got a TV around here?"

That's right, Tony thought. It was a Sunday in football season. "There's one in the den," he said. "Let's go downstairs."

But as soon as they got downstairs, Tony knew he'd made a big mistake. His father was in the den, sitting in his easy chair, watching the game.

"Uh, maybe we ought to go back upstairs," Tony said. The last thing he wanted was to remind Joel that his father worked for the nuclear plant.

"What's wrong with watching here?" Joel asked.

Mr. Cook looked up. "Sure, I don't mind the company."

Now it was definitely too late. "Uh, Dad," Tony said. "This is Joel Hinkie."

Mr. Cook stood up and shook Joel's hand. "Good to meet you. Have a seat." He pointed to the couch.

"Thanks, Mr. Cook," Joel said, sitting down. "What's the score?"

"It's Dallas by seven with five minutes left in the first quarter," Mr. Cook said. "I'm a Dallas fan myself. What about you, Joel?"

"Dallas all the way," Joel said.

Just wait till halftime, Tony thought.

When halftime came, Tony's father turned the sound down on the television. "I don't know about you, but halftime shows bore me to tears," he said. Then he looked at Joel. "You said your name was Hinkie?"

"Yeah."

"That names sounds familiar," Mr. Cook said.

"Well, uh, my mom is one of the leaders of the antinuclear movement here in town," Joel said.

Oh, no, Tony thought.

But his father only nodded. "Yes, that's where I've heard the name."

"You're the safety engineer over at the nuclear plant, right?" Joel asked.

"Well, I'm one of several," Mr. Cook said.

"My mother says that it's impossible to build a nuclear plant that's totally safe," Joel said.

"I guess that depends on what you mean by totally," Tony's father said. "Basically, a nuclear plant is as safe as the people who build it and maintain it want it to be. From what I can see, the Peekham plant is one of the best-constructed nuclear facilities in the United States.

As long as it's maintained properly, it should be safe for a very long time."

"Do you think it's being maintained properly?" Joel asked.

Mr. Cook seemed to hesitate for a moment. Then he said, "Well, uh, yes, of course it is."

"And what about the problem of disposing of nuclear wastes?" Joel asked.

"That is a problem that worries a lot of people," Tony's father said. "I think that in time it will be solved."

Tony was surprised by his father's answer. "You mean it's not solved now?" he asked.

"Well, steps are being made toward adequate disposal of nuclear wastes, Tony," his father said. "But, frankly, we're not there yet."

"If nuclear waste gets into the wrong hands," Joel said, "someone could build their own nuclear bomb with it. You could have all kinds of nuts running around with the bomb."

"But it's not that easy to make a bomb," Tony said, looking at his father.

"That's true," Mr. Cook said. "But it's not that hard either. We have to have safeguards against the misuse of nuclear waste. And against contamination, which will someday be an even bigger problem."

Tony was really surprised. Somehow he'd always thought that his father and the people at the Peekham plant had solved all the problems of nuclear power. Now his father was actually admitting that they hadn't It was hard to believe that they'd be fooling around with something so dangerous if they didn't already know all the answers.

"You know," Joel said to Tony's father. "You're a lot different than I thought you'd be. I mean, my mother says the people over at the plant are real maniacs who don't care anything about safety. I guess I should have known you were okay because you're a Dallas fan."

Tony's father laughed.

I can't believe this, Tony thought.

It was almost dinnertime when the game ended, and Joel said he had to go home. Tony walked with him to the front door.

"You know, your old man's okay," Joel said when they were out of earshot of the den.

"It's like I tried to explain in school," Tony said. "There really are two sides to this nuclear power thing."

But Joel shook his head. "You can think what you want, Tony, but most people still think nuclear power is too dangerous to fool around with."

Tony was confused. "But you just said you thought my father was okay."

"Yeah, I do," Joel said. "But what's that got to do with nuclear energy? All I meant is that he's a good guy. That doesn't mean I can't disagree with him. Even he admitted that they haven't solved all the problems of nuclear waste."

"I guess," Tony said.

Joel paused by the door. He seemed to hesitate. "Hey," he said. "Walk down the street with me, okay?"

"Why?" Tony asked.

" 'Cause I want to talk about something," Joel said.

Tony grabbed a jacket from the closet and went out with Joel. It was dark and chilly, and the smell of burning wood was in the air. For a while they walked without speaking. Tony couldn't imagine what Joel wanted to talk about, unless it had to do with nuclear energy.

"What's with Paul Smerman?" Joel asked finally.

"What do you mean?" Tony asked.

"I mean, how come he danced with Laurie all last night?" Joel asked.

"I guess he felt like dancing," Tony said. "After all, you took Randy. And you said you didn't care what Laurie did."

Joel stopped and looked at Tony in the dark. He seemed to have trouble finding words. "Yeah, of course I said that, Tony. What do you expect me to say in front of my friends? That I'm insanely jealous? The only reason I took Randy to the dance was to make Laurie jealous. Then Smerman stepped in and messed everything up."

For a moment Tony didn't know what to say. Joel had told him something intimate, a secret. By Tim's definition, that meant they were real friends. But Tony hardly knew Joel.

"I don't think it was really Paul's fault," Tony said. "He didn't know you were trying to make Laurie jealous. All he did was dance with her."

Joel seemed uncertain. "You don't think she really likes him or anything, do you?" he asked.

"I doubt it," Tony said. "I mean, Paul's probably my

best friend, but he's totally backward socially. I can't even get him to go out for a pizza."

"I don't know," Joel said. "He's a pretty surprising guy. Remember that touch football game? Who would have thought he had such great hands? And then last night he danced all night with Laurie. He wasn't a bad dancer, either. It makes you wonder."

Tony could see that Joel needed reassuring. It was true that Laurie seemed interested in Paul. But it still seemed impossible that she could be serious about him. Talk about Beauty and the Beast.

"Listen, Joel," he said. "I really don't think you have to worry about Paul."

Joel nodded. He seemed reassured. "Hey," he said, "I hope you'll keep this conversation to yourself, okay? I mean, this is just between us, right?"

"Sure, Joel."

Joel started to walk away. "See you at school tomorrow," he said.

Tony waved good-bye and walked back toward his house. He was almost in a daze. It was hard to believe that Joel had come over to his house, and hung out all afternoon, and then took Tony into his confidence. If that didn't make Joel his friend, he didn't know what did.

But now he had a real problem on his hands. Should he continue to encourage Paul to see Laurie, or should he try to help Joel get her back? And which one of them did Laurie like more? Tony knew there was only one way to find out.

16

When Tony got to Miss Crowe's class the next day Paul was already there, buried deep in his science book. Tony looked over his shoulder.

"Hey, you're three chapters ahead," he said.

Paul looked up. "So?"

"Why get ahead of the class?" Tony asked.

Paul shrugged. "Nothing better to do," he said, closing the book.

Hardly anyone had entered the classroom yet, so Tony leaned over toward Paul and spoke in a low voice. "Do you think Laurie really likes you?" he asked.

Paul sighed and looked up at the ceiling. He didn't answer.

"Joel Hinkie came over to my house yesterday," Tony said.

"So?"

"Well, what do you think it means?" Tony asked.

"It means that if you don't stop pestering me with these questions, Cook, I'm going to turn you over to the school psychologist," Paul said.

"I was only asking your opinion," Tony said.

"Why don't you ever ask my opinion on important issues?" Paul asked. "Instead of constantly bothering me with these idiotic questions? Who do you think I am? Dear Abby?"

"Am I imagining it, or are you in a bad mood today?" Tony asked.

Paul nodded. "My father has to take my mother to the doctor this afternoon, so I have to go to the store right after school and stay there until they get back," he said. "It's so futile. All I do is pick up the things that people knock off the shelves and try to catch little kids stealing candy. The fourth graders are the worst bunch of kleptomaniacs you ever saw."

So no one would be home at Paul's after school, Tony thought. That was just what he needed to know.

Now Laurie came into the room and sat down in her seat a few rows over from Paul and Tony. "Hi, Paul," she said, smiling.

"Uh, hi, Laurie," Paul said.

"Hi, Laurie," said Tony.

Laurie looked at Tony and scowled. "I didn't know you were in this class," she said.

Tony blinked. He'd been in the class since school started. How could she not have noticed him?

Laurie started talking to Paul again. "You know, my brother has a telescope, and when I got home Saturday night I asked him if he ever saw satellites. You were right. He says he sees them all the time."

"You can see some of them with the naked eye," Paul said. "Space is full of man's garbage."

"Don't you remember that day we talked about nuclear power?" Tony asked, interrupting them. "I said my father was a safety engineer at the plant and you said you didn't see how anyone could call nuclear power safe."

Laurie looked surprised. "Well, I guess I remember something like that."

"What is your point, Cook?" Paul asked.

But Tony just shook his head. He couldn't believe it. All this time he'd been convinced she wouldn't like him because of what his father did, and she *didn't even remember* what his father did. In fact, she didn't even remember that he was in her science class.

Laurie and Paul started talking again, and Tony turned away and opened his science book. It was pretty obvious that Laurie wanted to talk to Paul, not to him. But he didn't mind. He'd get to talk to Laurie later.

17

That afternoon Tony went straight from school to Paul's house. The house looked empty and the Smermans' car wasn't in the garage. He sneaked around to the back, pulled open the basement window, and slipped inside.

This time he managed to find the synthesizer without tripping over anything. He sat down and turned it on, reminding himself to keep an eye on the little red light. He dialed Laurie's number and waited for her to answer.

"Hello?" someone answered, but it wasn't Laurie. It was a man with a deep voice. Tony sat frozen at the speech synthesizer, not sure what to do.

"Hello?" the voice said again. "Who is this?"

Tony didn't answer. A moment later the man hung up.

Tony sat at the synthesizer for a couple of minutes, waiting. He figured he might as well try again. This time when he dialed the number, a kid answered. It was a boy and he sounded young. Maybe it was Laurie's little brother. "Hello?"

Tony decided to take a chance. He typed, and the synthesizer spoke in its electronic voice. *"Is Laurie there?"*

"Who's this? You sound freaky," the kid said.

"It's a bad connection," Tony typed.

"I'll say," the kid said. "You sound like a robot."

"You don't sound so hot yourself," Tony typed. *"Now, where's Laurie?"*

"I think she's outside. Can I take your number and have her call you?"

"Sure." Tony started typing out his phone number. *"Six, three, five, seven, five . . ."* Wait a minute! He suddenly realized what he was doing and stopped typing. He was giving away his secret identity. All Laurie had to do was call him at his house and she'd know who the mystery caller was. "You meatball," he said to himself, shaking his head.

"Yeah, six, three, five, seven, five, what?" the kid said.

"Forget it," Tony typed. *"Just go tell Laurie that Syn is calling."*

"Who?" the kid asked.

"Syn."

"Boy, not only do you sound weird, but you have a weird name too."

Tony looked up at the ceiling. Everyone had to be a wise guy.

He waited several minutes before Laurie got to the phone. She sounded breathless.

"Oh, hi, Syn," she said. "I'm sorry you had to wait so long. I was helping my mother plant winter bulbs, and I had to wash my hands."

"It's okay," Tony typed. He couldn't help being a little annoyed by how glad she sounded to hear from Syn. He wondered if she'd be as happy to talk if she knew who Syn really was.

"Did you go to the dance last Saturday?" Laurie asked.

"Yes."

"What color dress were you wearing?"

Tony scowled. *"I forget,"* he typed.

"How could you forget?" Laurie asked.

"Actually, I didn't wear a dress," Tony typed. *"I wore a blazer."*

"You did? Hmm. I looked pretty closely and I don't remember any girls wearing that," Laurie said. "I must have missed you."

"I guess," Tony typed.

"Did you have a good time?" Laurie asked.

"I had an okay time."

"I guess you know that I danced a lot with Paul Smerman," Laurie said. "I hope you're not mad. I mean, I didn't do it to make you jealous or anything. You're not mad, are you?"

"No."

"I was hoping you wouldn't be," Laurie said. "I don't know why I did it. It was fun and Paul was a good dancer, which was a nice surprise. But I think I just wanted to shock everyone, you know? Paul was so cute. Did you see the way he was dressed? It was so funny."

"Everyone was talking about you two," Tony typed.

"What were they saying?" Laurie asked.

"Just speculation. Like why you were with Paul and why Joel was with Randy."

"I'll tell you a secret," Laurie said. "Randy and I had a long talk about Joel on Sunday. It almost turned into a fight, but then we decided we liked each other more than him, so we both decided not to talk to him anymore."

"Do you really like Paul Smerman?" Tony typed.

"I don't know, Syn," Laurie said. "I didn't take him seriously when we started dancing, but then we talked about so many things. . . . I mean, he still seems kind of strange, but he's different too. I'm not sure I've ever known anyone like him before."

Tony sat at the synthesizer keyboard and sighed. The truth was he did feel a little jealous of Paul. He wasn't certain what he wanted to type next, and for a moment there was silence on the telephone line.

"How come you don't ask me about making friends anymore?" Laurie asked.

That was a good question, Tony thought. Probably because now that he was friends with Joel he wasn't as worried about it. But that reminded him of something. *"Suppose your father did something other people didn't like. Do you think kids would ever hold it against you?"*

"You mean, kids wouldn't like you because they didn't like your father?" Laurie asked.

"They might like him as a person," Tony typed, recalling what Joel had said about his father. *"But they might not like what he does for a living."*

"Like what?" Laurie asked.

Tony tried to think of an example. He didn't want to use his father's real job, of course. Then he thought of something. *"He might be a dentist."*

There was another long silence on the phone. Then Laurie said, "My father is a dentist."

Tony couldn't believe what a dummy he was. *"Oops, sorry,"* he quickly typed.

"But I guess I know what you mean," Laurie said. "I don't think anyone ever disliked me because of my father. You think that people don't like you because of your father?"

"Sometimes," Tony typed.

"What does he do?" Laurie asked.

Tony was tempted to tell her and drop the whole charade. But he was still afraid that Laurie would be really mad when she found out who Syn actually was. And if she ever told anyone about the mystery phone calls, he'd die of embarrassment.

"I can't tell you," Tony typed.

Laurie was just about to say something else when Tony heard someone calling her in the background. "Oh, that's my mother," she said. "I have to get off. But I want to tell you about my party on Friday night. It's a sleep-over party, but I'm inviting a few boys on the condition that they leave at ten o'clock. Would you like to come?"

"I don't know," Tony typed.

"You can tell your folks my parents will be there," Laurie said. "And if you want to stay over you have to bring a sleeping bag."

Tony smiled. It would be pretty funny if he showed up with a sleeping bag.

"You know, Syn," Laurie said. "I can't imagine what your father could do for a living that anyone would hate you for. I mean, even if he was an undertaker it wouldn't matter."

"We'll see," Tony typed.

"Okay, bye." Laurie hung up.

Tony turned off the synthesizer and climbed back out of Paul's basement. He wished he would be invited to Laurie's party. As Tony Cook, not Syn.

18

When Tony got home, he went into the kitchen to get something to eat. He found an apple in the refrigerator and was taking a bite when his mother walked in.

"Oh, there you are," Mrs. Cook said. "Someone just called you. A girl. I think her name was Laurie Rock or something like that."

The apple fell out of Tony's hand and hit the floor with a thud. Tony wondered if kids his age could have heart attacks, because if they could, he wanted one right away.

"What's wrong, Tony?" Mrs. Cook asked. "You look ill."

"Do you mean Laurie Stone?" he asked.

"Stone, that's right," his mother said, nodding.

"Oh, my God," Tony moaned.

"Tony, what is it?" Mrs. Cook asked.

"Is there a sharp knife around?" Tony asked.

"I suppose so, why?"

"Because I'm going to commit hara-kiri right now," Tony said.

His mother frowned. "Tony, I don't want you to talk that way. And pick up that apple."

Tony picked up the apple. There was only one reason why Laurie would call. Somehow she had figured out that he was the mystery caller. It must have been the part of the phone number he'd left with her little brother. Tony looked at the apple in his hand. Maybe he could smack it against his head and cause a fatal concussion. Or maybe he could swallow it whole and choke to death on it. Laurie knew! Why else would she call him? Tony felt ill. She must have been calling to tell him how much she hated him and how she was going to tell the entire grade that he had been making mysterious phone calls to her. He'd be the laughingstock of the school! No one would be caught near him. He'd never be able to go back to Peekham Junior High again! How could he face them?

The choices seemed clear. Either suicide or private school.

"Tony, what is it?" his mother said.

"Nothing," Tony said, slumping down into a kitchen chair. "Nothing a couple bottles of sleeping pills won't cure."

Mrs. Cook looked at him and shook her head. "You really are a character, you know that?"

Tony nodded.

"Are you in some kind of trouble?" his mother asked.

Tony shook his head. "Nothing that a sharp razor blade across the wrists can't solve," he mumbled.

"Tony! I don't want to hear any more of that talk," his mother said. "Now either stop it or I'll tell your father."

Something about mentioning his father helped Tony snap out of the total depression he was sinking into. There was no use running away. He had to face Laurie sooner or later.

He went to the kitchen phone and dialed her number. Then he turned to his mother. "You think I could have a little privacy?" he asked sadly. Mrs. Cook nodded and left the room.

After a few seconds Laurie answered.

"Laurie? This is Tony Cook."

"Oh, hi, Tony," Laurie said pleasantly.

"Uh, look, Laurie," Tony said. "I know why you called and I just want to ask you to try to understand."

"Understand what?" Laurie asked.

"Well, uh, why someone would do something like that," Tony said.

"Something like what?" Laurie asked.

"Er . . ." Tony was confused.

"Are you sure you're not mixing me up with someone else?" Laurie asked. "The reason I called is because I'm having a party on Friday night and I was wondering if you'd like to come."

For a moment Tony was utterly flabbergasted. Laurie was inviting *him* to her party? Then she still didn't know who her mystery caller was. A great wave of relief swept over him.

"Tony? Are you still there?"

"Uh, yeah." Tony could not believe that she was inviting him.

"You think you'll come?"

"Sure. Thanks, I'd love to."

"Oh, good," Laurie said. "And listen, you wouldn't happen to know if Paul Smerman is doing anything Friday night, would you?"

"I don't know," Tony said.

"Do you think you could do me a favor and try to get him to come too?" Laurie asked.

Suddenly the impossible became very possible to Tony. It wasn't him Laurie wanted at the party, it was Paul. She was just using him to get to Paul. "Well, you know, he doesn't really like to go to parties."

"I know," Laurie said. "But I thought that if you asked him he might come. You got him to go to the dance, didn't you? And you're his best friend."

"I guess," Tony said.

"Then would you try to get him to come to the party?" Laurie said sweetly. "I'd love to have both of you there."

Tony sighed. Going to Laurie Stone's on Friday night was better than not going. Even if he was simply a go-between for Laurie to get Paul to come. "Okay, Laurie, I'll try," he said.

"Great, see you then."

Tony hung up. Obviously Laurie was too embarrassed to ask Paul directly, so she was using him. But what was he? Paul Smerman's social director? So far, every attempt he had made at becoming popular had only helped Paul become more popular. It was ridiculous. If it hadn't been for him, Paul would still be a computer nerd! It just wasn't fair.

Tony looked at the apple on the table. Still, he did want to go to Laurie's party. So he'd better call Paul.

19

- -

"Laurie asked *you* to get *me* to come to her party?"
Paul asked after Tony called him.

"That's what I said, Paul."

"Why didn't she ask me directly?" Paul asked.

"I don't know," Tony said. "Maybe she was afraid
you'd say no. Maybe she figured she had a better chance
if she got me to ask you."

"Hmm, it's a tempting invitation," Paul said.

"Which means you'll go, right?"

"Well, not exactly," Paul said.

"What? Why not?"

"Because I'm not sure I want to."

Tony couldn't believe it. Who else in the world could
have an invitation like that laid at his feet and still
refuse?

"You're crazy, Paul. Nobody would refuse to go to
Laurie's party. I mean, you get invited to a party like
that and you become a member of the elite, the most
popular kids in the grade."

"Precisely," Paul said.

"I don't understand."

"Look, Cook, I've been thinking it over, and I really am happy being a computer nerd. The last thing in the world I need is to get caught up in the utterly insignificant world of adolescent intrigues and jealousies. So far I have managed to avoid all the silliness you seem so idiotically attracted to, and I don't intend to fall prey to them now."

"Tell me you don't think Laurie is pretty," Tony said.

"Well, I must admit she is attractive," Paul said.

"Tell me you wouldn't like to go out with her," Tony said.

"I suppose it might be interesting," Paul allowed.

"Then why are you being such a jerk?" Tony asked. "Isn't it obvious that she likes you?"

"No."

"Then why did she call me to ask you to the party?" Tony asked.

"Who knows? Maybe she wants me there to impress her friends with her worldly savoir faire or something," Paul said.

"And why did she dance every dance with you?" Tony asked.

"As I recall, Cook, there were only two eligible males at the dance who were as tall or taller than she, and the other one was Joel Hinkie, who was with Randy Kahn."

"Come on, Paul," Tony said. "Can't you give yourself some credit for once? Maybe Laurie really does find you interesting and different. Would that be so hard to believe?"

"Yes."

"You know what's wrong with you?" Tony said. "You have low self-esteem, Paul. You really do think that you're just a computer nerd. Why can't you see that you're more than that? You have . . . *substance*, Paul."

"You really think I have substance?" Paul asked.

"I think you're overflowing with substance," Tony said. "I think you're positively oozing substance." Just don't ask me what kind of substance, he thought.

"Really?"

"Why can't you believe that people might like you?" Tony asked.

"Because that's the way it's been all my life, Cook."

"But people change, Paul," Tony said.

"I haven't. I'm the same nerd I was in second grade," Paul said.

"But other people change, dummy," Tony said. "People who didn't like you because you wore funny clothes or were a brain in second grade don't think like that anymore. They've grown up enough to realize that clothes don't matter that much. And maybe they've begun to realize that people with brains can be interesting."

Over the phone Tony heard Paul sigh. "I'll say one thing for you, Cook. You are persistent."

"Then you'll go?" Tony asked.

"I'll think about it," Paul said.

Tony hung up, suspecting that Paul would agree to go to the party. It seemed as if he and Paul were finally becoming part of Peekham Junior High's social scene. It wasn't happening exactly the way he had wanted, but just the same, he was becoming friends with Joel and could probably become friends with Joel's other friends too. And he was invited to Laurie Stone's party.

Still, Tony didn't feel as pleased or excited as he thought he should. Maybe it was because he hadn't made friends the way kids normally do. Instead he'd done it by using Syn and Paul to help him. Maybe it was because he could tell that Laurie was just using him to get to Paul. He still got the feeling that she didn't care that much about him personally. It was like Tim had said—it was nice to have friends, but what counted was having a real friend. Now that he was getting to know Laurie and Joel a little, he could tell that they were nice, but when it came right down to it, he preferred Paul to be his real friend.

As he left the kitchen, Tony noticed that his mother and father were in the den talking in hushed voices. But as soon as they saw him, they stopped. His father looked pretty grim. His mother wasn't exactly all smiles either.

"Hey, what's up?" Tony asked.

"Nothing, Tony," his mother said.

But Tony could see that wasn't true. They looked too concerned over "nothing."

"Secret, huh?" Tony asked.

Mr. and Mrs. Cook quickly glanced at each other.

"Let's just say it's a private matter between your mother and me," Tony's father said.

"And I think it's time to start dinner," Mrs. Cook said, getting up. "Are Tim and Joyce home?"

"Joyce is," Tony said. There was no doubt in Tony's

mind that something was wrong. "Hey," he said, "everything's okay, isn't it?"

"Of course it is," Mr. Cook said. But somehow, sitting with his hands folded in front of him and his forehead wrinkled, he didn't look as if everything was okay. Tony could tell that they were keeping a secret from him, and he wasn't sure whether to make a big deal about it or not. He knew that there were other things his parents talked about that he wasn't supposed to know, either. It was all part of being a kid. But it sort of took the fun out of telling them about Laurie's party. It looked as if they had more important things to worry about.

20

The next day Tony stood in the cafeteria, waiting for Paul. But Joel arrived first.

"What are you waiting for?" Joel asked. "Let's get in line. I'm starving."

"Uh, okay," Tony said. Paul could catch up to them later if he wanted.

"I hear Laurie invited you to her party on Friday," Joel said as they moved through the lunch line.

"Yeah," he said.

"Smerman get invited too?" Joel asked as he reached for a chocolate pudding.

"Yeah. What about you?" Tony asked.

"Are you kidding?" Joel said. "Ever since the dance Laurie won't even talk to me. Neither will Randy. None of their friends will have anything to do with me."

Tony picked out a dish of raspberry Jell-O and whipped cream. "I bet they're just fooling around."

"You think so?" Joel asked as he pushed his tray toward the cashier.

"Sure," Tony said.

He and Joel paid the cashier for their lunches. "Let's go sit in the back," Joel said, heading toward the table where he and his friends always sat. A few minutes later they were joined by Dinks, who was carrying a tray filled with double helpings of everything. The overfed gorilla gave Tony an unfriendly look and sat down next to Joel. But he didn't say anything, because he was too busy eating.

"You think it's gonna be a big party?" Joel asked as they ate.

Tony shook his head. "She's just having some guys over until ten o'clock."

Joel scratched his head. "Boy, I still don't get it."

"Maybe she's trying to make you jealous," Tony said.

Dinks laughed. "How?" he asked. "By inviting *you* to her party?"

"I think she only invited me because she wants Paul to come," Tony said.

Joel glanced at Dinks. All of a sudden his attitude changed. "Aw, she's crazy if she thinks that inviting that nerd brain to her dumb party is gonna make me jealous. I mean, who cares? I'm tired of those dumb parties anyway."

It seemed to Tony that Joel had to put on an act in front of Dinks.

Joel looked at David and said, "We probably wouldn't go even if she invited us. Right, Dinks?"

"Depends on what kind of food she's serving," Dinks said as he devoured his second hot dog.

Joel rolled his eyes and looked back at Tony. "So you think Smerman is going to go?"

"Looks like it," Tony said.

Joel sat back and pretended he didn't care. "Well, she can have him."

Dinks finished his lunch and got up.

"Where're you going?" Joel asked him.

"I'm gonna get another lunch," Dinks said. "I feel hungry today."

"What else is new?" Tony asked.

Dinks glowered at him, but Joel laughed. When Dinks saw Joel laugh, he started to chuckle also. "You're a real funny guy, Cook," Dinks said. "A real funny guy."

Joel and Tony watched Dinks get back in the lunch line. As soon as he was out of earshot, Joel's attitude changed again. He turned to Tony and said in a low voice, "I thought you said you didn't think she was really interested in Smerman."

Tony shrugged. "I didn't think she was. But maybe I was wrong."

Joel shook his head sadly. "Man, you know you're in bad shape when the girl you like dumps you for a nerd like Smerman."

"Did you ever think that maybe Paul isn't such a nerd?" Tony asked.

"You mean because he's a good receiver?" Joel asked.

"And he's smart and he's a good dancer and girls like him," Tony added.

Joel shrugged. "I guess you're right. It's just that for so long the guy really was a nerd. It's hard to get used to the idea that all of a sudden he's the hottest stud on two feet."

Tony smiled.

21

_____

There was no Friday afternoon football game that week. Tony heard something about a game against some kids from another school on Saturday instead. It still bothered him that no one had asked him to play, but then, Joel and his friends hadn't been invited to Laurie's party, either. It seemed like an even draw.

Friday night after dinner Tony pushed open the bathroom door and found Joyce inside, putting on makeup. Tony started brushing his hair.

"Another antinuke concert?" he asked as he watched his sister. She put on so much makeup, it seemed as if she were painting a new face on top of her own.

"There's a meeting at Mrs. Hinkie's house," Joyce answered. "And what are you doing? Going out with Paul again?"

"We're going to a party at Laurie Stone's house," Tony said proudly.

Joyce stared disdainfully at her younger brother. "Don't you ever get tired of your hedonistic life?" she asked.

"My what?" Tony said.

"Your hedonistic life," Joyce said. "All you're interested in is parties and dances and having a good time. Did it ever occur to you that there are important things in life? If the world was filled only with people who were hedonists like you, we probably would have all suffocated from smog or been blown to bits in a nuclear war a long time ago."

Tony studied his sister in the mirror. "Hey, Joyce, can I ask you a question?"

"What?" his sister replied as she applied eyeshadow.

"Are you really against nuclear power or are you just into it because it's the in thing at school?" Tony asked.

"There are a lot of kids at school who couldn't care less," Joyce said. "But I think it's very important."

"Then how come every time you go out to do something with the antinukers you have to get all made up?" Tony asked.

Joyce sighed. "I don't see what one has to do with the other, Tony. Just because I'm against nukes doesn't mean I can't wear makeup."

"Unless there's some boy antinuker you're interested in," Tony said.

Joyce glared at him. "You really make me ill, Tony. You have this totally perverted view of girls. You think the only thing we care about is guys. Well, it just so happens that it's not true. And maybe someday when you grow up you'll learn that."

"Well, *excuuuse* me," Tony said.

Joyce looked back at the mirror. "I'll tell you something else, Mr. Chauvinist Hedonist. Have you noticed how Dad's been in a bad mood lately?"

"Yeah," Tony said.

"Do you have any idea why?"

"Uh, not exactly."

"It's because starting in about two weeks he's not going to have a job at the nuclear plant anymore."

"What?" Tony said.

"You heard me," Joyce said.

"What do you mean, he's not going to have a job?" Tony asked.

"Why don't you go ask him?" Joyce said.

That's exactly what Tony decided to do. He went downstairs and found his parents in the kitchen. Mr. Cook was having a hot chocolate, and Tony's mom was working on a crossword puzzle.

"Hey," Tony said to his father. "Joyce says you're going to lose your job."

His parents looked at each other.

"How come you told Joyce and not me?" Tony asked.

"We planned to tell you tomorrow," his mother said. "We thought you'd want to go to the party tonight and enjoy yourself."

"Well, now that I know, will you tell me?" Tony asked.

"Sure, have a seat," his father said.

Tony sat down. He noticed that neither his father nor his mother looked very upset.

"It's pretty simple, Tony," Mr. Cook said. "The Peekham Nuclear Power Plant is actually three nuclear generators clumped together, and they supply energy to this whole region. Over the last few years, the company that runs the plant has noticed that the demand for energy has been dropping. I guess people just aren't using as much electricity as the utility expected. Anyway, last week they decided that they can get by on just two of the three generators. And that means they don't need as much staff as they used to."

"But how come you're getting fired?" Tony asked.

"It's a seniority situation," his father explained. "Those who have been there the shortest time are the first to get laid off."

"But we think we've worked out some alternatives," Mrs. Cook quickly added. "You don't have to worry about moving. We still plan to live here for a while."

"What are you gonna do?" Tony asked.

"There's a lot of new construction out here, and I think I can do some consulting work," his father said. "If that goes well, I may even open my own engineering firm."

Tony nodded. His parents seemed pretty calm about the whole thing. It might have just been an act so that he wouldn't worry, but Tony couldn't tell. Just then, the front door bell rang.

Tony got up. "That must be Paul."

He opened the front door. There was a kid standing outside. He looked sort of like Paul, except that his hair was cut and combed neatly, and he was wearing jeans and a new beige crew-neck sweater and sneakers.

"Hi, Cook," the kid said, using Paul's voice.

"Paul, is that you?" Tony asked. "You look great!"

"Really?"

"Hey, would I kid you?" Tony asked.

"Yes," Paul replied.

"I swear, Paul, you really look good," Tony said. "I mean, you even cut and combed your hair."

Paul seemed uncomfortable. "Well, are you ready to go?" he asked.

"Uh, wait, Paul," Tony said. He wasn't certain he really wanted to go to the party now. Not after what his parents had just told him.

"Maybe you ought to go ahead without me," he said.

Paul looked shocked. "What? Are you insane? I couldn't possibly go to that party without you."

"Sure you could," Tony told him. "The only reason I was even invited was because Laurie wanted you to come. You don't need me."

Paul's composure seemed to crumble. "Don't do this to me, Cook," he begged, his voice growing panicky. "You said from the start that we were in this together. I can't go to that party alone."

Tony heard someone behind him and turned to find his mother coming down the hall.

"Hi, Mrs. Cook," Paul said.

"Oh, hello, Paul," Tony's mother said. "Don't you look marvelous."

Paul blushed. "Uh, thanks, Mrs. Cook."

"So you're off to the party?" Tony's mother asked.

"Well, I wasn't certain I should go," Tony said. "I mean, considering Dad and everything."

"Oh, don't be silly," his mother told him. "Of course you should go. Everything is going to be fine."

"You sure?" Tony asked.

"Absolutely," Mrs. Cook said.

"Well, okay, just let me go get my jacket." Tony went to the front closet.

"Don't be home too late," Mrs. Cook told him as he went out and she closed the door behind him.

"Is something wrong with your father?" Paul asked.

"I'll tell you about it on the way," Tony said. He and Paul started to walk to Laurie's house.

22

It took about ten minutes to walk to Laurie's house, and all the way there Paul jabbered nervously.

"Do you think there's going to be dancing?" he asked.

"If there is, you don't have to worry," Tony told him. "You did fine at the dance last week."

"But that was in the gym, and this will be in Laurie's house," Paul said.

"So what's the difference?" Tony asked.

"There's a difference," Paul said firmly.

Tony couldn't believe it. He'd never seen Paul act this way.

"What are you so nervous about?" he asked. "I thought you didn't care about things like parties."

"You're right. I don't," Paul said. But a few seconds later he said, "Who do you think will be there?"

Tony sighed. "Just figure they'll be the most popular kids in the grade."

"You don't think we'll look foolish?" Paul asked.

"If you keep acting this way, you sure will," Tony told him.

"I can't help it," Paul said.

Laurie's house was different from all the others on her street. While the others were tall, boxy, traditional-looking houses, Laurie's was low and modern-looking. Dr. Stone must have been a pretty successful dentist.

Tony stopped at the foot of the driveway and looked up at Paul. It was funny, the way things had changed. Paul was so nervous, and he felt so calm. Everything was backward.

"Listen," Tony said. "You have to stop being so nervous. That's part of the trick. You have to act like you've been going to parties like this all your life. You can't act like you're surprised you're here. You have to act like you'd be surprised if you *weren't* here."

Paul nodded and glanced nervously at Laurie's house. All the lights were on, and they could hear music coming from inside.

"But they know we haven't gone to parties before," Paul said.

"That's just what I've been trying to tell you," Tony said. "If you act like you have, then you have. Now come on, let's go have a good time." He turned and started walking toward the house.

"Wait," Paul said.

Tony stopped. "What now?"

"Do you really think Laurie likes me?" Paul asked.

Tony smiled. "You mean as more than someone just to dance with and talk to?"

Paul started to blush. "You know what I mean."

"But, Paul, I thought you didn't care about things like that," Tony said.

Paul turned redder. "Well, in this particular instance I might make an exception."

"I guess we'll just have to see," Tony said.

Paul got angry. "Cook, I need help. Can't you tell me anything?"

Tony laughed and grabbed Paul's arm and tugged him toward the house. "All I can tell you, Paul, is that you're not going to be graded. With girls, it's strictly pass or fail."

Tony rang the door bell and Laurie opened the door. She was wearing jeans and a red-and-white-striped sweater, and she looked really pretty, as usual.

"Oh, hello, Tony. Hello, Paul," she said graciously. "I'm so glad you could come."

They went in. The inside of the house was beautiful. Tony and Paul followed Laurie down into a large sunken living room where everyone was gathered. Along one wall was a table with bottles of soda and trays of hors d'oeuvres. Arnie Tregger, the class vice-president, was across the room, chatting with Bobby Adler, whose father was supposedly one of the richest men in Peekham. Stephanie McKearny, the cheerleader, was sitting on the couch with Wendy Wright, the class president. And Mia Newmark, the number-one singles player on the girls' junior high tennis team, was sitting with them.

Randy Kahn was there, too, and around the room Tony spotted several others who until tonight he had only glimpsed occasionally in the school halls.

Laurie told them to help themselves to some food, and they wandered over to the table and poured a couple of glasses of Coke. They also had some pigs-in-blankets, small egg rolls, and potato chips.

Meanwhile, Paul looked around nervously. "What do we do?" he whispered to Tony.

"We mingle," Tony whispered back as he chewed on some chips.

"With whom?" Paul asked in a low voice.

"With the people who are here, dummy."

"But I've hardly ever talked to any of these people before," Paul said. "Except during tests when they wanted to know answers."

Tony looked around. To tell the truth, he'd never talked to any of these people, either. He knew you had to start somewhere. Only he didn't know where or with whom to start talking. Everyone else at the party seemed to know each other already and seemed to be talking to someone else.

Tony turned back to the snack table. "How about some more Coke?" he asked.

Paul nodded and Tony refilled their cups.

About five cups of Coke and a few dozen hors d'oeuvres later, Laurie finally came to their rescue. "Come on," she said, pulling Paul by the arm. "If I don't get you two away from the food, we'll run out by eight o'clock." She led them over to a couch and sat down with Paul. There wasn't really room for Tony, but he managed to squeeze in next to Paul anyway. This pushed Paul even closer to Laurie.

"So, Paul," Laurie said. "You never told me where you learned to be such a wonderful dancer."

"Uh, my older sister used to practice on me," Paul explained.

Tony was surprised. "You never told me you had a sister you danced with."

"Well," Paul replied, "I didn't think it was the kind of thing you went around bragging about."

"You really are full of surprises," Laurie told Paul.

Paul shifted uncomfortably and cleared his throat. "Not really."

"What about that football game?" Laurie said. "I'll bet no one thought you'd catch those touchdown passes."

That's for sure, Tony thought.

"I was just lucky," Paul said.

"This sure is different," Laurie said. "Finding someone who's modest for a change. Why do you think guys who like science and math seem to be more modest than, say, guys who like sports?"

"Well, for one thing," Paul said, "you spend a lot of unexciting time in the lab doing tedious experiments or at home working on math problems. It isn't very glamorous."

"But still, the excitement of making a scientific breakthrough," Laurie said. "It must be thrilling."

Oh, give me a break! Tony thought. He wasn't sure whether Laurie was acting like a total phony or was just trying to make conversation. Either way, this was one conversation he wasn't interested in. Besides, Laurie was paying attention only to Paul. Tony decided to get up and stroll away.

For a few minutes he wandered around. Even though a lot of the popular kids were there, the party itself wasn't quite what he had imagined it would be. Arnie Tregger and Bobby Adler were in the den, playing with Laurie's little brother's home video game. Stephanie McKearny and Mia Newmark were putting braids in Wendy Wright's hair. The party seemed much less interesting than he'd expected. Tony paused and leaned in the doorway. Well, he had finally made it in. The question was, into what?

Suddenly there was a commotion near the windows by the front door, where Laurie and Paul and a couple of other kids stood, pointing outside. Tony went over and looked. Outside he could see a group of four or five guys standing in the dark.

"It's Joel and his friends," someone said.

"Well, he's not invited and he's not coming in," Laurie said.

"It doesn't look like he's leaving, either," Arnie Tregger said.

"Someone has to go out and tell them to go away," Laurie said. Tony noticed that Bobby Adler and Arnie Tregger were suddenly crouching down out of sight behind the couch.

"Tony," Laurie said, "tell them to go away."

"Me?" Tony asked, suddenly wishing he too had hidden.

"Yeah, Tony," Bobby Adler said, looking up from the couch. "You tell 'em."

"Why me?" Tony asked miserably.

"Why not?" Arnie Tregger said as he and Bobby pushed him toward the door.

The next thing Tony knew, he was standing in the dark outside Laurie's house. A dozen yards down the driveway Joel and his friends were standing around. Tony took a deep breath and started walking toward them.

"Hey, look, it's Cook," David Dinks said.

"Uh, hi, guys," Tony said. As he got closer he recognized Carmichael and a couple of others.

"Hi, Tony," Joel said. "You think Laurie will let us in?"

"It doesn't look promising," Tony said.

"What do you mean, promising?" Dinks asked.

"I mean she sent me out here to tell you guys to go away," Tony explained.

"Oh, yeah?" Dinks said, and stared at the house.

"Listen," Tony said quickly. "I don't know why you'd want to go in there anyway. It's pretty boring."

A couple of guys laughed.

"We could liven it up a little," Carmichael said.

But Joel turned to his friends and said, "Listen, you guys stay here and don't do anything dumb. I want to talk to Tony for a second."

They walked across the street until they were under a streetlight and out of earshot of the rest of the guys.

"Listen, is Smerman in there with Laurie?" Joel asked.

Tony nodded.

Joel shook his head. "Jeez, I don't get it. What does she see in that guy?"

"Maybe she's just bored and wants to meet some new people," Tony said.

Joel was silent for a moment. Then he said, "That's funny. Sometimes I know exactly how she feels."

Now Dinks and the other guys approached them.

"Let's get out of here, Joel," Dinks said. "I feel like getting something to eat."

Joel nodded and looked at Tony. "You want to come with us?"

"I would, but I guess I better hang around the party," Tony said.

Joel nodded. "Okay. But listen, there's a touch football game up at school tomorrow against some guys from Stonefield Junior High, if you feel like playing. And tell Smerman he might as well come too. We could use a good receiver."

"I'll tell him," Tony said. "See you guys later."

Joel and his friends left, and Tony walked back to the party. It was so ironic, he thought. Not only had he been invited to Laurie's party, but Joel had finally asked him to play football too. The weird thing was, now that all this had happened, it didn't seem like such a big deal after all.

Back inside Laurie's house, everyone wanted to know what had happened.

"They just wanted to know if they could come in," Tony said.

"What did you say?" Laurie asked.

"I told them they couldn't," Tony said.

"And that was it? They listened?" Arnie Tregger asked.

Tony nodded.

"Our hero!" Bobby Adler yelled.

"The Alamo is safe for another night," Arnie Tregger added.

A couple of kids laughed, but Laurie smiled at him. "Thanks, Tony," she said.

Everyone went back to what they had been doing before Joel and his friends had arrived. Tony sat on the steps leading down to the living room and just watched. A couple of times he glanced over at the couch where Paul and Laurie were sitting, lost in conversation. It was weird how things had worked out. He and Paul were at the party and Joel and his friends weren't. But it didn't seem to matter much either way. Maybe his sister was right after all. Maybe popularity wasn't so important. He half wished he was outside fooling around with Joel. Maybe you just always wanted what you didn't have.

"You look bored," someone said.

Tony looked up and found Randy Kahn standing next to him. She was very pretty, with beautiful fiery red hair and blue eyes and freckles. She was also much closer to his height than Laurie.

"Not bored," Tony said. "Just thinking."

"About what?" Randy asked, sitting down next to him on the step.

"Nothing." Tony grinned at her.

"Sometimes I get lost in thought too," Randy said, smiling back.

"Oh, yeah? What do you think about?"

"Well," Randy said, "I look at that couch and I wonder how Paul Smerman ever got to be such a good-looking, fascinating person."

"That's funny," Tony said. "I was thinking the same thing."

"Maybe some people are just late bloomers," Randy said.

"Could be," Tony said.

"Or maybe they have a friend who makes them come out of their shell," Randy said.

"That might be true too," Tony said.

"But what's sad is that sometimes that friend gets left out," Randy said.

"Oh, it's no big deal," Tony said. "I'm sure the friend can handle it."

"I hope so," Randy said. "Because I'm sure the friend is interesting in his own way too."

Tony looked at Randy and smiled. "Hey, I hear your father collects racing cars."

"Yes, he does," Randy said.

"I really like that kind of stuff," Tony said. "How about you?"

Randy shrugged. "Oh, it's okay," she said. "What's really fun is when he takes me for a ride in one of his old cars. Everywhere we go people stare at us."

"Is that because of the car or because you're in it?" Tony asked.

Randy giggled and blushed a little. Tony decided he really liked her blue eyes.

"He doesn't have any Formula One racing cars, does he?" Tony asked.

"I don't think so," Randy said. "What are they?"

"They're the most beautiful racing cars in the world," Tony said. "And they race on the most beautiful tracks in the world. Like Le Mans and Watkins Glen and Monte Carlo. And the guys who drive them are the best racing drivers in the world."

Randy Kahn leaned her elbows on her knees and looked up at him. "It sounds fascinating, Tony," she said. "Tell me more."

23

It was late when Tony finally got home. It seemed as if he had talked with Randy for hours, and his throat was dry and sore. But he couldn't have been happier. He wasn't certain, but he got the feeling that Randy liked him. At least she was interested in him. And she'd invited Tony to come over and look at her father's cars anytime he liked!

Tony let himself into the house quietly. Sometimes his parents went to bed early on Friday nights, but there was a light on in the den, and he heard typewriter keys tapping. He went in and found his father at the desk.

"Oh, hi, Tony," Mr. Cook said, glancing at his wristwatch. "How was the party?"

"It was good, Dad." Tony nodded at the typewriter. "What are you doing?"

"Just writing up some consulting proposals," his father said.

Tony sat down on the arm of the couch near the desk.

"Are you sorry that you have to leave the plant?" he asked.

Mr. Cook leaned back in his chair and thought for a moment. "I guess I'm a little disappointed. But they're giving me a lot of severance pay, which is a decent thing to do. And I've always wanted to try consulting, so it's not the worst thing in the world. Besides, I always figure that it's better to look at what's ahead rather than dwell on what's already passed."

Tony understood. "You know," he said, "a couple of weeks ago I would have been really happy about you leaving the plant. I used to think that the kids around here didn't like me, because you worked there. But now I don't think it matters."

Mr. Cook seemed amused by this. "Is that so?" he said.

"Yeah. Remember that kid, Joel Hinkie, who came over and watched the Dallas game that day?" Tony said. "The one whose mother is the head of the antinuke movement here? Well, he said you were a good guy, especially since you're a Cowboys fan."

"Tony, I'm glad to know that," Mr. Cook said.

"I just think it's good that people will give you a chance, even if they don't like what your father does for a living," Tony said.

Mr. Cook nodded. He was smiling.

The next morning the phone rang early. Tony slept through it until his mother knocked on his door. "Tony, phone for you."

He rubbed his eyes and looked at the clock. It was

8:45. Who called at 8:45 on a Saturday morning? He got out of bed and went downstairs to the kitchen to the phone. "Hello?" he said, yawning.

"Do you think it's possible that Laurie really likes me?" Paul asked.

"Paul, it's eight forty-five in the morning," Tony said. "So?"

"So I'm still asleep," Tony said, yawning again.

"Tony, this is important!"

"So is my sleep," Tony said.

"But I don't know what to do," Paul said.

"Boy, I wish I had your problems," Tony told him. "The most popular, most intelligent, most beautiful girl in the grade likes you, and you don't know what to do."

"But I don't," Paul insisted. "I mean, what if she wants me to kiss her?"

"Well, then you kind of push your lips together and close your eyes and aim for her lips," Tony said.

"But I've never done it before," Paul said.

"Then practice in a mirror," Tony told him.

"What?"

"Go look in the mirror, Paul. You'll see a face. Then pretend to kiss that face."

"You're not serious," Paul said.

"Well, you can also practice with a pillow. That's what my sister used to do."

"Kiss a pillow?" Paul said.

"You can even draw a face on it," Tony said.

"Cook, I'm serious," Paul said. "I think she expects me to do something, take her out on a date or something, and I'm petrified. I always help you with your math. How about helping me?"

"Okay, I'll tell you what," Tony said. "Maybe you and me and Laurie and Randy will do something together. Would that make you feel better?"

"Infinitely."

"Good. Now don't forget that Joel wants you to play touch football today."

"I can't," Paul said. "I have to go to school this morning to set up my speech synthesizer for the science fair. And the judging is this afternoon. Can you beat Stonefield without me?"

"Give me a break!" Tony said, and hung up.

24

On Monday morning Tony, Joel, and David Dinks stood around waiting for Miss Crowe to start science class. Joel was telling Tony how Dinks had broken his all-time eating record at the mall the night before.

"Four deluxe burgers, four large bags of fries, and four thick shakes in fifteen minutes," Dinks said proudly.

"The human trash disposal," Tony quipped.

Joel chuckled. Dinks scowled and then grinned. "Hey, that's funny."

"I hear that Randy has been asking about you," Joel said.

"What does she want to know?" Tony asked.

"You know, the regular stuff," Joel said. Then he smiled. "Between you and Smerman, a guy doesn't stand a chance."

Before Tony could reply, Miss Crowe came in and started class. As usual, the first thing she said was, "Does anyone know what day it is?"

Hands started going up, and Miss Crowe called on students.

"The first day of the rest of your life," someone said.

"Yes, but no."

"Albanian Independence Day?"

Miss Crowe shook her head.

"The anniversary of the first man on Mars?"

"We've never put a man on Mars," Miss Crowe said.

"Then someday this may be the anniversary," someone said.

Miss Crowe rolled her eyes. "All right, now who is going to give me a serious reply?"

As usual, Laurie Stone's hand went up. "It's the first day of the science fair."

"That's right," Miss Crowe said. "So why don't we all go down to the gym and take a look?"

The science fair took up the whole gym. As Miss Crowe's class entered, Tony saw that there were several other science classes already there. The projects were set up on tables in long rows, and next to each project was its exhibitor, who was spending the day in the gym explaining his or her project to the classes that came in. Miss Crowe's class began to look at the projects, and Tony walked with Joel. Laurie was about thirty feet ahead of them.

"This kind of stuff doesn't turn me on," Joel mumbled low enough so only Tony could hear.

Tony nodded. "Know what you mean."

"So, listen," Joel said as they walked. "You feel like coming over to my house after school today?"

"Sure," Tony said.

Ahead of them a large group of students were gathered in front of one of the projects, and Tony and Joel stopped to look. It was Paul's speech synthesizer, and on the table beside it was a large blue first prize ribbon. Paul was sitting behind it, explaining how it worked.

"It will say whatever I type on the keyboard," he said. Then, to demonstrate, he typed on the computer and the synthesizer said, *"I am a speech synthesizer built by Paul Smerman."*

Various members of the crowd gasped in amazement and Paul smiled proudly.

Tony noticed that Laurie had a funny look on her face. "Paul, could you try something else?" she asked.

"Okay," Paul said.

"Try 'Hello, this is your mystery caller,' " Laurie said.

Paul started typing and the synthesizer said, *"Hello, this is your mystery caller."*

"Just amazing," someone said.

"Yeah, unreal."

"I think it's an excellent project," Miss Crowe said. "Congratulations, Paul."

Paul grinned. "Thanks, Miss Crowe."

Miss Crowe and the class moved toward the next project, but Tony noticed that Laurie had stayed behind. He also stopped a little ways down the aisle. "It was you," Laurie said.

Paul looked confused. "It was?"

"Why did I think you were a girl?" Laurie asked.

"Me? A girl?" Paul asked, totally bewildered.

"It never occurred to me that you could be Syn."

Paul took a step backward. "Syn?"

But Laurie just smiled. "Oh, it doesn't matter now, Paul. I just think it's sweet. All this time you liked me, but you were too shy to let me know." She stepped close and kissed him.

"Uh, uh . . ." Paul was speechless.

"I better catch up with Miss Crowe," Laurie said. "Would you like to come to my house after school?"

"Uh, okay."

While Laurie caught up with the class, Tony stood next to Paul and the synthesizer.

"So, how did it feel to kiss Laurie Stone?" Tony asked.

Paul frowned. "Good, but how could she think I was a girl?"

"Don't worry about that," Tony said. "Just think about going over to her house after school."

"I guess I'll have to skip my computer club meeting," Paul said.

Tony looked up at him. "Don't you realize that you're not just a computer nerd anymore? I mean, now that you've cut your hair, you're good-looking. You wear nice clothes. You get invited to the best parties and touch football games, and the prettiest, smartest girl in the grade just kissed you and invited you to her house after school."

Paul nodded. "It seems that you're right, Cook."

"For once, I *know* I'm right," Tony told him.

"It's just that I don't feel any different," Paul said.

"That's because you're *not* different," Tony said. "You never were a computer nerd to begin with. You just thought you were."

Paul smiled and straightened the collar of his new crew-neck sweater. "So you think I'm pretty hot stuff, huh?"

Tony just sighed.

CELEBRATING
YEARLING
25 YEARS

Yearling Books
celebrates its
25 years—
and salutes
Reading Is
Fundamental®
on its 25th
anniversary.